"Madam, are we acquainted?" he asked, little caring if he offended by not remembering her identity.

"Oh, intimately." She laughed at the shock he could not hide. "I gather I have changed a great deal since our last encounter. Everyone does, I suppose."

"Madam, I don't believe that it could be true that we've met before," he complained, irritated by her game. "You're the sort of woman a man would commit to memory. Presumptuous."

"Presumptuous? Yes, well, my father said that about me often. He said I embarrassed him," she replied, and then shrugged. "He also said you would not appreciate my sense of humor. But I only ever teased you as much as you would tease me."

No
Duke of
Mine

HEATHER BOYD

"NOW, Jasper. Here is a list of everything I want done while I'm away," Algernon Sweet murmured. "If the weather permits, get them all done as quickly as possible. Otherwise, some of the more complicated matters can wait until my return."

Jasper flicked through the three pages. "Are you sure this is enough for the two weeks you'll be away?"

"Well, there are four more pages in my desk drawer if you have too much free time," he complained.

Jasper glanced over at his wife, Sophie, who was waiting to bid Algernon goodbye as well, and grinned. "No chance of that happening, now I'm a married man."

Algernon laughed at him. Jasper was smitten,

and it showed. He had liked his brother's wife before their marriage, and now even more so.

Now that his brothers were all together at Ravenswood, it was easy to see that all his siblings were happy in their marriages, albeit in different ways. They hadn't been in such good spirits since their childhood. But now that his brothers were settled, he had things to do without their involvement.

He had a woman to woo and marry, expenses to be repaid that were pressing on his conscience, and somewhere in there, he fervently hoped he could find some joy in his endeavors.

Making a marriage because you are forced to it for the money was quite different from choosing to do so of your own free will. His brothers had been very lucky not to have shared his burden.

"Your Grace," Nash called as he ran into the entrance hall. "One quick question. Do you mind if I borrow the globe for the children's lessons?"

He sighed in relief that his request was nothing serious. "No, I do not mind."

"Good, good. It'll be back in its place by the time you return, I promise."

Algernon highly doubted that. Everything that went through his brother's new apartment seemed to never come back immediately. There was always some excuse for taking a book from the library again, and some reason for the delay in its return.

Nash was determined that all of his children were properly educated on every matter under the sun, but thankfully, his wife was prone to ferrying the children outside when something did not come naturally to one of them. The young family played a great deal, for which he was grateful and proud. Algernon had a hand in making Nash and Laura get along again, and much better than before.

"Your Grace, you are late leaving," Laura Sweet, his sister-in-law, complained with a smile on her lips and an hourglass in her hand. "Your carriage has been standing outside for the last fifteen minutes, and your men and horses are growing restless out there."

Lady Laura Sweet often commented about his tardy behavior, which he probably deserved. He'd harassed her to sit and fix her marriage to Nash, and now she felt justified in bossing him about.

But she was right. He'd dragged his feet more in the last six months making this decision since inheriting the title than he had in his entire life. He held up his hands in mock surrender rather than admit that out loud. "I'm going, I'm going."

Her eyes narrowed. "That is what you said yesterday, and the day before, and the day before that. I'm starting to think you can't bear to be parted from us."

"The London season could arrive before he does, at this rate," Jasper teased. "Do you want the carriage put away again?"

"No."

"Do you think we should travel with him? Make sure he doesn't get lost or waylaid," Stratford asked, adding his voice to the harassment.

"Yes, all right, I am going today. I'll be back in exactly two weeks."

Laura drew close and gently laid her hand on his sleeve. "We'd come with you for moral support if you want us to, you know."

"I know." If his family came with him to London now, though, he might as well ring every bell in London to announce that the Duke of Ravenswood was in pursuit of a bride. "I can do this alone."

"As you wish, but remember we're only a letter and a fast horse away," Laura promised, patting his arm. "We'll prepare the duchess' chambers discreetly while you are gone as well, so don't worry about that."

Algernon may be a duke, but in a house full of women, he had discovered that he rarely had to worry about the running of his home. This was, perhaps, a kind of preparation for the day when he was a married man. His wife would rule the roost, and he would not even be told of what she might do. His duchess would make all the decisions for the household in the future.

Nash returned, baby Isabelle in his arms and his sons hard on his heels. "Aunt Violet wishes to speak with you before you leave."

"Again? Damn her. What now?"

"It's your own fault for trying to keep this trip a secret from her," Nash explained.

"Seymour probably told her. There will be no secrets left in this household soon," he complained. But Algernon squared his shoulders. "Best see what the old dragon wants before I go."

The last time he'd been summoned like this, the dragon had insisted he make haste to marry. He fully intended to if he could ever leave the estate.

He found Aunt Violet in the morning room, tea, a London newspaper, a pile of fresh correspondence at her elbow, and *his* butler waiting to do *her* bidding.

She squinted at Algernon. "About time, boy."

"You wanted to see me, Aunt?"

"Yes," she said, and then glanced at the butler pointedly.

She did not tell him to leave, but it was clear she wished to have a private word without the butler listening in. "Seymour, would you be so kind as to have the coachman walk the horses again? I will be there as soon as I can, and we can be on our way."

When he was gone, he glanced at his aunt with a brow raised. "We're alone now."

She gulped. "I have a favor to ask of you."

"Beyond giving our butler an assistant of his own?"

"I should like you to dismiss him from your service," she announced. "Dismiss Seymour today, before you leave."

Algernon gaped. "I cannot dismiss him. Seymour is essential to the running of the estate, especially when I am away. I thought you liked him."

She huffed. "Oh, I do. Just not as a servant."

Algernon stared at her in confusion. Her expression seemed vexed, and then he noticed her cheeks turning red. Embarrassment? The suspicions about his aunt and butler suddenly had her request making a strange sort of sense. "You like my butler, but not as a butler."

Her eyes flashed with an emotion he'd never seen there before. *Fear.*

He and his aunt were not close. She criticized him and how he ran the estate constantly since her return. However, he was not her enemy, and Algernon debated how to reassure her of that. "What can I do?"

"Do what I want."

"I cannot, but perhaps I could simplify matters upon my return." He paused. "I will be making a call to the Archbishop of Canterbury to obtain a special license to marry Lady Kent while I am in London. Perhaps I could secure a second for you."

Her eyes widened. "Yes, that is what I want most of all."

He nodded. "Consider it done, Aunt."

She let out a shuddering breath and smiled hesitantly. "Safe journey, boy, and a fast return."

He bowed and swept from her presence, bemused that he was about to play matchmaker again when he returned to Ravenswood. A marriage to a butler for a noble-born lady was bound to make waves in society and in the family. But if he approved, others would not be difficult.

Surely, having two very old people marry respectably was better than sneaking around after dark to see each other and risking broken bones.

He found everyone waiting at the front door still, even his butler. He gave the older man additional instructions. "Keep a close eye on my aunt."

"Yes, of course," Seymour promised.

"Make sure she doesn't become too tired with the children sitting on her knee," he warned. "Shoo them away and lock the door."

"There is no stopping her when it comes to the young ones," Seymour told him.

"Find a way to keep her happy until I come back," he insisted.

Algernon nodded to everyone else, took one last glance around him, and sighed heavily. There was nothing left to keep him from his duty now. No reason to delay in the hope of a last-minute rescue from marriage. All his instructions had been delivered and would be executed in his absence.

Algernon climbed into his carriage, resigned to leave at last. Sims, his valet, was there already. Once Algernon was settled, he waved to his family, and the driver set off for their destination.

A stack of papers was immediately passed to him—a first draft of a marriage contract between himself and Lady Stephanie Kent to review.

He was sure she would say yes. He was certain he would get the money he needed from her. And he was also positive that she would have a great many demands and would want changes made to the contract, despite his diligence.

He went through each page for at least half an hour each, studying them intently, willing the time he needed to spend in the carriage to fly by.

The fastest he had ever traveled to London was four days and four nights, stopping at coaching inns, hotels, or the homes of friends along the way. This time, he intended to make the journey nonstop, changing horses at each posting house before proceeding on.

It was an insane rush, but given how much he had left behind at home to do, he still needed time to woo Lady Kent when he got there.

"I don't like the look of that," his valet mumbled, breaking into his gloomy thoughts sometime later.

Algernon glanced at the man opposite and noticed the direction of his gaze. His valet's face was fixed toward the horizon. Algernon looked too and saw dark clouds in the distance. Perfect.

He hated traveling in the rain. He hoped those clouds stayed far away.

But within an hour, the carriage and horses were pelted by a heavy fall, and their speed slowed as the horses struggled with the suddenly slick roadway.

Algernon and his valet had to brace themselves as they careened down a steep hill that led to a crossing. The banks were already licking at the roadway as they crossed, but they made it through without incident and pressed on to the next posting house. Knowing that the bad weather could change to good in an instant, he resumed his study of his papers.

But just as they reached a small village, the rain came down even harder still. The inn was shut up against the wild weather, and they pressed on for the next bridge.

"It's getting bad out here for the men and horses, Your Grace," the coachman called down.

He checked his pocket watch. They hadn't traveled nearly far enough for the first day, but there was no excuse for mistreating horses or men.

"Keep going," Algernon shouted up to the coachman. "If we can clear the next bridge, we'll stop for the night at the first village after that."

"Right you are, Your Grace," the coachman answered, cracking a whip over the horses' heads.

The next bridge was old, made of stone but low. They should have no trouble crossing it in normal conditions, but the carriage pulled to a rough halt.

"It's underwater," the coachman called.

Algernon poked his head out the door, cursing as he was instantly soaked. The chill seeped quickly through his shirt to his skin. "How deep do you think?" he yelled, to be heard over the drumming on the carriage roof.

"Above the axle."

That wasn't good for the horses. They were already struggling, and the water would be bitterly cold this close to winter. Losing even one horse would be disastrous for his plans.

Suddenly, there was a great blinding crack of

lightning, and the horses jerked the carriage sideways, tossing Algernon out the doorway. He landed face-first in a river of cold mud and muck.

He cried out an oath and sprang to his feet, but the horses, spooked by a lightning strike, plunged toward the bridge, dragging the broken carriage—and his men—along with them.

CHAPTER TWO

"GOOD DAY TO YOU, SIR," Maggie Black called, pushing her way to the front of the line of travel-weary people so the innkeeper at the Stag noticed her. "Excuse me, I require a room for the night."

"You and everyone else, stranded because of this accursed bad weather," he complained. He looked her up and down, frowning, and then peered past her, searching the crowd. "I'll speak to your husband first."

Maggie had no husband, no companion, either. "Sir, I can pay you well and want only a small room and bed," she promised, raising her chin. She shifted her traveling trunk slightly behind her, so he wouldn't notice the shabby state of it.

Maggie could not help the lack of a husband. But her aloneness was a situation that had made other innkeepers nervous along the way, and, oddly, her traveling companions found it disagreeable, too.

They also seemed to believe her untrustworthy, since she enjoyed a good argument.

She could not help her journey, as she was traveling to meet her papa, not that it was anyone's business but her own. The last she'd heard, her father had taken up a new position near London, but she hadn't heard from him since. That had been months ago.

As usual, he'd gone to work for a wealthy family, and what funds she had scrounged together for the journey to find him had to be carefully doled out until he gave her more.

She haggled lightly with the innkeeper for the cost of a room only. But it was more than she'd expected to pay in the end. Her money would not last long at this rate, but every innkeeper on this road seemed willing to rob their customers blind, and unless she wished to sleep in the stables, she had to pay what they thought was fair.

Maggie could have given her father up as a lost cause long ago, but she had never quite been able to. She'd made a foolish promise to her mother as a girl that she would always, always, heed her father's wise words and do as he said.

But that had become hard, since he gave back so little warmth in return.

She placed money on her side of the counter and waited impatiently for the man to make his decision and accept her coin. She hoped he would assume her to be an irritable sort of female and agree just to be rid of her.

He looked her up and down and nodded, and she pushed the money the rest of the way toward him. He pocketed it quickly. "You can wait in the private dining room where it's warm and dry until your room is ready," he offered.

Maggie was relieved. "Thank you, sir."

He immediately started speaking to the next person in line, and Maggie fled. A dry, comfortable night was all she required, and she hurried into the private dining room, glad for a few moments of peace and solitude after the difficulties of the day.

She headed toward the rain-splattered window to look out, and noticed that the bad weather was not letting up. Thunder rolled overhead and lightning flashed, blinding her temporarily. Maggie drew back from the window and blinked until her vision cleared. She'd overheard the inn's servants warning other guests that the storm could worsen tonight. That seemed very likely, too. The road beyond the front of the inn was a quagmire of mud and filth.

She'd heard enough complaints upon her arrival to know that more road-weary travelers could be expected soon. The roads surrounding the village were known to flood because all rivers and streams nearby tended to break their banks all at once. So she was lucky to have secured a room for tonight. But she could be here for days if the bad weather continued, and she hoped her funds did not run out.

She worried even more about anyone still out there in the storm when another crack of lightning shook the ground the little inn stood upon.

She had just pulled out a book from her pocket to check its condition when a married couple entered the dining room with a flurry of anxious words and reassurances that the storm would pass. The pair glanced her way, commented upon the foul weather, but kept a distance, hovering near the fire instead, flicking water off their traveling cloaks.

Maggie observed the pair discreetly. She could tell they loved each other deeply by the way they fussed. Love, patience, and consideration were writ large over their faces, and she envied them such a settled life.

Maggie checked her own attire discreetly. She was not so much wet as damp all over. During her journey today, she'd invited a young child to perch on her lap to spare a tired mother juggling two. The mother had been grateful, and for that short time, Maggie had pretended that the child was really hers. But when they were gone, she'd buried the yearning for motherhood and a family as usual because it hurt too much to think she might never have that.

She would have to wait until she had the privacy of a bedchamber before she attempted to dry her gown, cloak, and boots. She had been unlucky to be given a carriage seat on the edge of the bench and had traveled by the door, where the bad weather and rain had seeped through.

She devoted her attention to her book again, and let the couple converse with each other.

As half an hour passed in waiting, Maggie fretted that the innkeeper had given her room away, and fought a shiver. When he finally arrived, all gruff and apologetic about the wait, he took the married couple away first, promising to return momentarily for Maggie.

She walked to the fire, holding her hands out to the warmth of the flames, slightly disappointed since she'd been first to wait for her room. But as she stood there fighting her impatience, she became aware of raised voices beyond the private dining room.

Curiosity drove her across the chamber to the door to see what the commotion in the taproom was all about.

When she opened the door a crack and put her eye to the gap, she instantly spotted a new group of men standing about, dripping water all over the taproom floor.

They were cross and road-weary, and obviously caught out by the storm. The leader was arguing with a servant, demanding rooms and food for them all immediately.

Maggie could feel the man's frustration from where she stood, sensed too that he was used to getting exactly what he wanted, when he demanded it, and it had better be the best on offer. Likely a wealthy man, unused to the hardship of difficult travel, despite his bedraggled appearance.

But whoever he was, he was in for a very, very rough night. Maggie suspected the inn would not have enough rooms for everyone in need who stopped here. It was not that large an establishment.

The fellow started toward her.

"Sir, please, you can't go in there. There's a lady inside. She should not be disturbed by men in such a state."

Maggie froze, her eye still peeking through the gap as attention turned toward the private dining room door. The tallest among them glared in her direction, clearly seeing her silhouette through the partly open door. He muttered something she could not hear but instinctively understood. He had cursed—and Maggie opened the door wider, incensed by his lack of manners and rude speech.

They stared at each other for a long moment. But then...something about his curse, the mud on him, the shape of the jawline under that drooping felt hat, tweaked her memory.

She concentrated only on the taller fellow of the group as he continued to glare, compelled to challenge him for some reason.

She felt she knew him. From where, she could not say yet. He was not a recent acquaintance but someone from her past, someone from long ago.

Maggie had met many young men as her father practiced his profession. Of course, if it were long ago, he would have been a great deal shorter, but he had been equally filthy, wearing mud and muck, and in a temper then, too.

Maggie stifled a laugh as his identity became clear.

Dear God, she had stumbled upon Algernon Sweet, up to no good. Covered in mud and just as cross about it again.

It had been such a long time since she'd seen her father's old pupil, or seen him in such a disgraceful condition. Of course, the last time had been entirely the fault of his ego, but given the weather today, she did not think he was entirely to blame for his current state.

He took a pace toward her, eyes flashing anger, but it seemed very likely he had not recognized her. That was a great disappointment, because Algernon had been unforgettable...and her only friend once.

She became aware of the innkeeper speaking to her.

"I beg your pardon," Maggie murmured, turning her attention to the man.

The innkeeper looked between her and Algernon, frowning severely.

But even before he opened his mouth, she knew what he wanted from her. To leave the taproom and his patrons immediately. The taproom was no place for a proper lady.

"I trust my room has been made ready, sir," she said with a haughty tilt of her head.

"It is. If you will follow Mrs. Roper now," he said firmly, glancing into the taproom once again.

She nodded, her eyes returning to Algernon once more. She seemed to have captured his interest now, because a small smile was playing over his lips.

She winked at him. "Well, I had best depart so these road-weary travelers can claim the private dining room."

"Thank you," the innkeeper said, as his wife arrived looking harried and tired.

She escorted Maggie away into a hall and toward the staircase leading to the upper floors.

Mrs. Roper stopped and faced Maggie. "I apologize for my husband's surly manners just now. We get all sorts here, but I can see you'll be no trouble."

"Of course not."

"I also hope you were not offended by the gentleman's boldness in the taproom, either. It's been a terrible day, and everyone is in a bit of a temper over the lack of accommodation."

"I do understand, and I'd advise you leave your husband to deal with that particular gentleman, if I were you," Maggie said—and then gasped and looked around, "Oh, one moment please!"

Maggie dashed back into the private dining room, glad the room was still unoccupied, to where she had left her travel case and snatched it up.

She rushed back out of the room as she heard the heavy tread of boots approaching. She slipped back into the hall unseen, but paused to listen to her once-upon-a-time friend take possession of the chamber and start giving out orders.

She noticed his voice was deeper, but he complained a lot more about the bad weather than he used to at twelve. As he urged his men to dry off, a shiver raced over her skin that had nothing to do with being damp and cold, or his concern for his servants. "Make sure the horses are rubbed down and have the carriage wheel looked at. I hope to be away from here at first light."

She grinned. Algernon had been in a tearing hurry every day that she'd known him, except when he was reading a book in the library with her. She had often teased him that he'd miss something important if he did not slow down.

But she would do no teasing of him anymore. He was important, and she was no longer a child of his tutor's, running nearly wild through a grand house and on the manicured grounds with him. Algernon was wealthy and destined for a dukedom, being the oldest son and heir, and Maggie might have become a dutiful wife at best, had her father provided a dowry for a woman at her advanced age of six and twenty.

She climbed the stairs, following the innkeeper's wife, glad to know her old friend was still largely as she remembered. But Algernon might not want to see her again. Not after the trouble she'd caused him that last day at Ravenswood. Now that she was older, she understood better the scandal that could have erupted over her growing friendship with a duke's son and heir.

Their stations in life had been extraordinarily different, as were the expectations for their futures and behavior. The laughing boy she'd known, Algernon, had been destined for greatness, while Maggie's station in life continued to sink lower.

She entered her rented room and withheld a sigh. Barely a closet with only a small window set in the wall. There was no fire, but the room felt surprisingly warm. Besides a single bed—a plain wooden box—an aged mirror hanging on the wall, and a pair of candlesticks, it was bereft of embellishment.

"You're against the chimney from the kitchen, so you should be right cozy in here tonight. Hang up your wet things on the pegs on that wall and they could be dry by morning," the woman promised. "There's another pair of blankets in that box at the foot of the bed, and I'll send up something warm for your supper later."

"I did not pay for supper," Maggie confessed, wincing.

"I can see you've fallen on hard times, love, and it's all right. My husband will never know."

Although she was surprised by the offer of charity, she wasn't so proud as to refuse a meal. But all she really wanted was to dry her clothing and sleep the night away.

The innkeeper's wife rushed off, promising to

send up warm water to wash with in the morning, and then left Maggie to deal with the remaining travelers downstairs.

Maggie locked the door and began to remove her damp outer garments, eager to be rid of them. She hung her cloak and gown on the pegs and pressed her hands against the warm brickwork. With luck, her clothing might be dry enough to put back on before the promised dinner tray arrived.

Maggie removed her footwear and wrapped a blanket around herself before going to the tiny window. Her chamber overlooked the road, and the river that wound around through the small hamlet could be seen and also offered her a glimpse of those who arrived. She craned her neck to look farther afield. There was not much to see until a carriage being pushed and shoved came into view. It was being directed toward the side of the inn, where the stables were likely situated.

The carriage was clearly damaged as it was listing to one side rather badly, held up by a handful of struggling men. She winced as she thought of the dripping-wet lord downstairs, a viscount when she knew him, and how his poor servants fared, too. Algernon's carriage must have broken down on his journey to somewhere important. He was either coming from London or going to it, similar to her situation, she supposed, and that was unfortunate. It seemed like the worst luck to be traveling the same road this week.

She turned from the window and considered getting into bed and staying there. But as she caught sight of her reflection in the square of mirrored glass hanging crookedly on the wall, she nearly died of embarrassment on the spot.

Her bonnet was a limp wreck, she had a black smudge on her cheek and nose, and some of her dark hair had escaped its moorings on one side of her head. Worst of all, the damp weather had made it stick straight out.

She was the most bedraggled woman in existence, and so embarrassed. No wonder the married couple had kept a distance, or that Algernon hadn't recognized her. Maggie looked like she was headed for Bedlam.

CHAPTER THREE

ALGERNON GLARED out the front door of the taproom. "Would you look at that? Would you just look at that? Will this infernal rain never end?"

"Not according to the innkeeper," his valet warned, shivering beside the taproom fire, unwilling to give up his spot.

The rain had been coming down hard since yesterday, great sheets of it, obliterating the view and turning the road into a never-ending stream.

Algernon was irritated. He was still damp, and he was tired, having not slept well last night due to the lack of available rooms. A chair in the dining room was all very well for a light doze, no more than an hour, but it was a soft bed he craved under him at night.

At least he was clean again, and more presentable.

But with the rain coming down and the roadways flooded, there was no chance of any room becoming available anytime soon. The other guests could hardly leave, or want to share their chamber and bed with a stranger.

Although if that pretty woman from yesterday showed her face again, he might be in luck. He'd been hoping to spot her again, but she'd taken supper in her chambers last night and, to his disappointment, remained abovestairs still.

He turned back to the taproom. The locals had gathered around the room and were silently sipping ale and talking amongst themselves. Algernon listened discreetly, thankfully ignored for now.

"This is nothing compared to the flood of seventy-four," an old man said.

"Oh, the one of eighty-eight was much worse," another argued. "Trapped for nearly a month that time."

Algernon tried not to groan.

Sims leaned toward them. "Did the bridge wash away completely?"

"No, not the bridge. The roads that led up to it washed away, though. Took forever to get our side done, and then the other side took their sweet time, too."

"Brilliant," Algernon said under his breath. "That's all I need to hear."

He might never reach London at this rate, and he might not be able to return home by Christmas, either.

Another fellow came in, and Algernon realized, judging by the way he looked around, that he was not a local but one of the few guests who had secured a room upstairs.

The man came his way. "Dashed nuisance, all this rain, isn't it? The name is Keane, Charles Keane."

"Allan Sweet. Yes, a great nuisance indeed," Algernon agreed.

"Ah, well. Glad I've got my wife with me for company." The man chuckled. "It would be a dull few days without the conversation of my family, wouldn't it, sir?"

Algernon agreed with him. When he traveled, he usually had a brother with him. Most often Nash, but he would go nowhere without his wife and children these days. Jasper was needed to run the estate in his absence, and Stratford, while Algernon adored him, would have blathered the whole way to London. He had his valet, of course, but traveling with a servant paid to agree with you was not the same at all.

Algernon normally preferred to travel light and as inconspicuously as possible anyway, without using his title, but he regretted that now. A duke could have commanded the best room in the inn, had he looked like one upon his arrival.

"And the other woman traveling with you is comfortable upstairs, too, I suppose?"

"Other woman? I have no—oh, you're talking about the young lady in the chamber beside ours, aren't you? Yes, yes. You must be. Quite a retiring little thing, but handsome. Haven't seen a peep of her since we first arrived, though."

"I saw only a glimpse," he said, hiding the truth. Algernon had been unable to tear his eyes from her face.

"A widow, I suspect," Keane continued. "My wife is very disapproving of her staying in her room so much. Barely spoke a word to us yesterday, and the woman kept her nose in a book the entire time. My wife prefers conversation to reading when we travel."

Algernon's hopes soared. An amenable widow traveling alone might be interested in a gentleman's company after dark. And bookish women had always appealed to him. "I have yet to meet this particular lady."

"Hasn't she come down yet again?"

"Not that I've seen." And he'd been looking for her, too, and anything else to divert his attention on such a gloomy, damp day.

"This bodes well for a lively dinner this

evening, then." Keane grinned. "You'll have to tell me what you make of her after your first meeting."

"Perhaps," Algernon said, but he usually guarded his opinions of others for those who deserved to hear them.

"Now, I know I should go up and check on my beloved wife soon, but I think an ale is in order first. Will you join me?"

"Indeed." Algernon ordered an ale for them both and sat with his back to the view of the road, deciding that as long as he could hear the rain, there was nothing else to see outside.

He was nearly done with his first tankard when a small figure appeared in the distant dining room, whose doors had been left open to allow others to freely use the space to stretch their legs. She paused in the doorway and looked out into the taproom, and their eyes met again.

Algernon felt a jolt of recognition. The same as he had yesterday. But he couldn't imagine why he thought he knew her.

He leaned across to the other guest and asked, "What was the lady's name?"

"I don't know that I ever heard it. We were in a bit of a state yesterday and eager to reach our room. Introductions were not performed, I'm afraid." He shrugged. "Perhaps my wife could find out for you. I could go upstairs and ask her."

The woman suddenly beckoned him to join her in the dining room.

"No, that's quite all right," Algernon said quickly, immediately rising to his feet, irrationally compelled by that small, demanding hand to obey. "Do excuse me, Keane."

The fellow muttered something in response, but Algernon's whole body was fixed on meeting the bookish widow who could hopefully enliven his day.

He hurried towards the dining room, entered the space and, on instinct, shut the door behind him.

The widow was at the window, her back to him. She had dark hair and a nice figure—somewhat shorter than him—and was well-dressed. Well...reasonably well-dressed. She was obviously not a wealthy widow.

She turned slowly. "Did your carriage break down?"

She was a bold one, this widow, and Algernon liked that in women. "Yes," he said, edging closer in the hope of identifying her voice before she noticed his confusion. "Before we could reach the next bridge, in fact."

"Ah. It is a great shame the rain did not hold off for one more day. We might have all made it through unscathed. Or was it providence that it rained when it did, forcing you to slow down for a change?" she asked, raising one brow.

Algernon was intrigued. Most women did not immediately speak to him like this, as if they were accustomed to casual conversation with him. The title conferred on him as a young man had set him apart for most of his life. His elevation to duke had created a formality with people he had known for years.

He drew closer, sizing her up. Yes, a little on the short side for his taste. She had a pleasant round face, intelligent, deep brown eyes, and, if he was not mistaken, an appreciation for *his* figure, too, given how her gaze drifted over him.

His scalp tingled when she glanced up at his hair and grinned. "Have you lost your hairbrush?"

He quickly raked his fingers through it and heard her laugh softly.

"Still vain, I see."

But the sound of her laughter was pleasant, rather than mean-spirited, and he knew he'd heard that laugh before. He just couldn't say from where still.

"Madam, are we acquainted?" he asked, little caring if he offended by not remembering her identity.

"Oh, intimately." She laughed at the shock he could not hide. "I gather I have changed a great deal since our last encounter. Everyone does, I suppose."

"Madam, I don't believe that it could be true that we've met before," he complained, irritated by her game. "You're the sort of woman a man would commit to memory. Presumptuous."

"Presumptuous? Yes, well, my father said that about me often. He said I embarrassed him," she replied, and then shrugged. "He also said you would not appreciate my sense of humor. But I only ever teased you as much as you would tease me."

He drew back, staring at her. "I enjoy a good jest as much as the next man, but women do not taunt me unless they are prepared for the consequences."

"Are you dangerous now? Or do you despise females as much as your father used to?"

"I'm not dangerous unless it is to a lady's virtue." He promised. "My father never understood that the feminine intellect is not so different from our own."

"I'm surprised you would admit that, since you once claimed your sex possessed a greater intelligence." She smiled, her eyes sparkled with unconcealed mirth.

She was enjoying his confusion immensely.

Algernon tilted his head to one side, looking her over again. She was known to him. Something about her was off, though. He could almost put his finger on what it was. Since she wore gloves, Algernon could not determine if she wore a wedding ring or jewels on her fingers yet.

"I have stumped you. How delicious. You always claimed to be so good at riddles, though I'm sure you will tell others that you figured it out much sooner than you will."

He glanced to the side, to a dining table, and detected a book with a pair of spectacles sitting on top. Neither one gave him a clue. Many women read and wore spectacles.

He scowled. "There's something wrong with how you look, madam."

"There is nothing wrong with me, Fair-bridge," she claimed, setting her hands on her hips and glaring at him with annoyance.

Algernon drew closer, challenged rather than put off. He'd been a duke for most of the year now, so she was not a new acquaintance but an older one who did not know of his elevation. "It is Duke of Ravenswood now, madam. My father died."

"Oh," she said quickly, setting a tiny hand to her chest. "My humble apologies, Your Grace. News travels slowly to my part of the world."

He raised a brow. "And what part of the world would that be?"

"Now that could be giving you every clue if

you ever knew where I'd gone," she said, waggling her brows. "You will eventually remember who you are dealing with and become cross with yourself that I bested you again."

That, too, was familiar.

The woman stood there, smiling up at him, slightly swaying, making her rather plain gown shift around her legs, her eyes sparkling with laughter.

He clicked his fingers multiple times. "It's just there. I can almost taste it."

She wet her lips, and Algernon stared at them, too.

"By that look, I assume you are thinking a kiss might help your memory," she murmured. "I wonder if that could be true."

If he'd known her as intimately as she claimed, they surely would have kissed. This was hardly the privacy he usually sought, but, well, with his siblings properly married, someone had to set a bad example these days.

Algernon bent his head and captured her pretty lips, hoping to spark some long-forgotten memory.

But the kiss only confused him more. Her inexperience was obvious, but she still kissed him back, and with unexpected enthusiasm. He explored her mouth, enjoying her like a fine wine he'd forgotten he'd enjoyed sampling before.

Rich, all-consuming. The kind you could lose your soul for.

And Algernon could not get enough.

He framed her face with his hands, finding new angles as he extended the kiss well beyond the bounds of propriety. Her tongue teased against his, and he sucked it gently into his mouth.

When she withdrew, he followed, unable to stop himself from becoming aroused by her kiss.

When he felt a subtle pressure against his chest, he heeded reason and drew back a little, astonished at himself for getting so carried away in a room with no locks on the door.

The woman seemed momentarily dazed, her lips parted and her breathing rushed, but then she grinned. "You've improved."

But still, he had no newly recovered memory of her, and an overwhelming desire to kiss the woman again and perhaps more, all night long. He crowded her against the window a bit, settled his hands on her hips, and held her there, studying her face in earnest.

The woman bore his proximity and scrutiny without fear or complaint, but a bright blush climbed her cheeks, signaling that she was affected by him, and he drew back again, puzzled by how he could have possibly forgotten having such a passionate woman in his arms before.

"My dear Algernon, I had forgotten how easy it was to lead you by the nose. I could always get you to do what I wanted."

He paused, staring at her hard as he remembered the only person, a mere slip of a girl, who had held that power over him. Who had bested him more than once and called him by his given name. But they'd been children then. Him barely twelve and her ten, and thrown together for so short a time. Short but entirely memorable.

No wonder he was having so much trouble identifying the woman before him.

Bookish Maggie Black had grown up into a remarkably provocative woman.

But a bucket of cold water had been dumped over his lust, now he knew who he was dealing with. She had tricked him into a kiss today. In the past, it had been a mutual decision to learn to kiss with each other. But those days should have been left far, far behind.

Well, if she wanted a game, he'd play along— and he would make her squirm just as much in return for tricking him.

"Lady Sally Ford," he said, snapping his fingers and enveloping his long-lost friend in his arms. "I could never forget the passion of your kisses."

CHAPTER FOUR

"CLEARLY, you have a mind like a steel trap, Your Grace," Maggie said sourly, after a long moment.

Algernon laughed and drew back, grinning at her unhappy expression. "Maggie Black, you deserved that for teasing me."

The woman smiled back cheekily. "Algernon Sweet, Duke of Ravenswood. I'm pleased to see that the weight of your new responsibilities hasn't robbed you of your sense of humor, such as it was."

Algernon enveloped her in a long hug again and rocked her from side to side, caught in a wave of relief at seeing her once more. Maggie had been a good friend once, before her father had taken her away from Ravenswood when his tenure as tutor had abruptly ended. He and Maggie had shared secrets, studied forbidden subjects, and laughed together, often at his brothers' many follies, for the whole of a year.

They had kissed, too, practicing on each other in secret. But those kisses had lacked the passion they'd just shared, of course. He'd always thought of her as a near sister then, and had missed her funny ways.

He released her slowly and looked down into her face, adjusting to the changes time had brought. Her eyes were a warm, deep brown, glowing with the kind of knowing light that an eager man might get lost in now. Her eyebrows delicately arched in question at his continued scrutiny, and he tweaked her nose as he'd always done, making her smile brighter.

He looked beyond her face to her glossy black hair, tied neatly at the back of her head today. Gone were the unruly curls she had forever tried to tame after running about the estate, following him and his younger brothers.

Now that she'd grown older, she possessed more curves, poise, and elegance than the bookish girl of whom he'd been so fond. A woman like Maggie would no longer be running off into fields with him, or risking getting into trouble with her father by sneaking out of bed to meet him in the dead of night.

But then he remembered where they were, her father, and her unknown marital status. For all he knew, she could have a husband waiting nearby.

That thought sobered him, and he drew back to a respectable distance. He glanced around, but thankfully, they were alone. He wet his lips, still nervous. "Maggie, is your husband with you? And I should dearly love to renew my acquaintance with your father, as well," he blurted out quickly.

Maggie lowered her gaze. "I never married, and my father is...somewhere...near London."

He was taken aback that she had not married, until her last words struck a wrong chord. "Somewhere? Don't you know where your father is?"

"Not precisely. That is why I am on my way to find him," Maggie confessed, and then shrugged. "I have not had a letter from Papa in some time, and I am growing concerned that something may have befallen him."

Algernon sat on the edge of the table so they were of more equal height, barely believing that Maggie was a spinster. "How did you become separated from Mr. Black?"

"I haven't traveled with him in years. Not since..." She hesitated. "Well, the reason isn't important."

Algernon remembered her father being a pompous old windbag. Forever suppressing Maggie's natural curiosity while toadying up to Algernon's late father. Mr. Black had not approved of his daughter's close friendship with his employer's eldest son, and had locked her in her attic room more than once.

Fortunately, Algernon was able to acquire the housekeeper's key, and they all kept that a secret from their elders.

"So your father and you fell out, and seriously this time."

"I chose to make my own life," she announced, bristling. "My father continued as he preferred, as well."

Algernon sensed a vast deal left unsaid about her father. He knew better than to push, though. Maggie would tell him, or not, in her own sweet time. "So your father continues to teach?"

"Oh, yes. He devoted his life to serving the finest minds in all of Britain and helping them achieve greatness."

Algernon's breath caught at the bitterness in her tone. "Did he never help you do the same?"

She stared at him briefly, and then laughed. "No. Of course not. I'm only a woman, and not worth taking pride in. But he's often written to tell me about the fine young men he was leading to their grand future."

"You beat me in every test, despite being two years younger!" Algernon burst to his feet, infuriated by her father's lack of attention on her behalf. He gripped her shoulders and squeezed. "The finest mind he ever tutored was *yours*."

"He would never admit that a daughter could surpass his own precious students, and risk his career," Maggie said, her voice dripping with contempt. But then she shook off whatever ill temper gripped her. "Are you traveling to London or going home to Ravenswood?"

He sat back down so they were of similar height once more. "I'm on my way to London, or was until the weather got in my way."

"The nerve!" She moved to sit beside him, leaning against the table too. "I never had the opportunity to visit London."

"That is a great tragedy," he mused, shifting sideways until he nudged her. "There are many fine bookshops there that you would enjoy. Perhaps you'll visit them with your father when you find him."

"I doubt I shall ever see London's bookshops. My purpose is only to discover how my father fares."

"Ah, yes. And with this rain, of course, your journey to him is delayed like mine is."

"Indeed." She pulled a face. "I should rather not have to make any journey at all in such dreadful weather."

"My thoughts exactly."

She squinted at him. "How did you come to be so covered in mud yesterday?"

"You saw me? Oh, yes, that was you spying on me in the taproom? Inquisitive as always, I see, but why didn't you speak to me then?"

Maggie shrugged. "You seemed in ill temper, so I thought it best to avoid you."

"I was frustrated. Exhausted. We were soaked through and shivering. I am still damp. The effort to right the carriage and drag it back to this place had put us all in a bad mood. I did my part. Helping the men, though they didn't want to let me at first."

She laughed softly, imagining the odds of success for anyone else changing his mind. "The last time I saw you, you were in a similar condition and your father was cross. I think that is the only reason I picked you out. That, and your outrage at not getting a room for the night."

"Yes, and I foresee another uncomfortable night ahead of me, given that the rain continues hard still, so no one can leave."

"Ah, well, there is little I can do about the rain." She glanced over at him and suddenly hugged his arm. "But perhaps I could share my pillow with you."

His brow rose high. Slightly surprised to hear an invitation to share her room. And her bed, too? "I don't think that's a wise idea."

She winked at him. "It wouldn't be the first time you snored on my pillow."

"I do not snore," he protested, as he always did when someone complained about it.

Maggie only laughed, and Algernon found himself smiling back. Her good humor had always been an antidote for a bad day as a boy. It seemed to work miracles on his mood today, as well.

She sighed. "I found it a rather comforting sound, actually. That and our conversations before bedtime. I still have an interest in philosophy, so you could fall asleep almost immediately if we ever start talking about that."

He grinned. "So you still study?"

"Not as much as I would like to. I have developed my own philosophies, but I have no one to discuss them with at home."

"I should very much like to hear how you view the world, and debate philosophy all night again," he promised.

Maggie hugged his arm and then released him. "I'm sure you're much too important to be burdened with my company or opinions anymore."

He captured her hand. "I never was bored with you. I'm certain nothing has changed."

She snorted, then a knock sounded at the

door and she sprang away, putting a respectable distance between them.

"Yes, come in," Maggie called.

Maggie was no shrinking violet, but she was no brazen flirt, either. She cared about her own good reputation, and he ought to worry about it more, too.

The older man he'd met earlier in the taproom entered the dining room, with a woman of equal age hanging on his arm. The pair glanced at them suspiciously.

Algernon smiled quickly. "Imagine my surprise at finding it was my cousin staying in this establishment," he said smoothly.

The pair glanced at Maggie, eyes wide with surprise.

Maggie seemed lost for words for a long moment, but swiftly recovered and shrugged. "He vexed me the last time we talked, so I didn't share my plans to travel with him."

"Maggie," he chided. "You are family, and I will follow you everywhere, my dear."

"I had hoped you'd grow out of that nonsense," she muttered to him, smiling, but the next moment she excused herself from the room.

Although Algernon wanted to follow immediately, the gentleman and his wife got in his way. Mr. Keane brought his wife closer and introduced her.

"A pleasure to meet you, sir," the lady gushed. "I must confess to having been very worried. It is not right for a woman to travel alone. You must have been so worried about your cousin as well, to follow her into this dreadful storm."

Algernon nodded slowly. "She's always had an independent disposition."

"I am glad you've come to take charge of her."

"I have indeed," he promised, but of course, he had not. However, talking with Maggie was an excellent way to spend a rainy day and night. He would like to continue their conversation elsewhere. "Any idea which room was given to her?"

The Keanes were only too happy to supply him with directions to the room beside theirs.

Algernon rushed up the staircase and knocked softly on her bedchamber door.

"Yes," Maggie answered from behind the wood.

"It's me."

"What does *me* want?"

"I thought we might discuss sharing your pillow tonight," he whispered urgently. "Let me in so we can talk freely."

"One moment."

There was near silence from within, but when the door opened, something was thrust out at him. The door slammed shut again without him catching a single glimpse of Maggie, before the bolt was thrown to keep him out for good.

Algernon held what he'd been given up to the light—and gaped. He held a small embroidered pillow bearing Maggie's initials. He stared at it, and then at the door in consternation. "Maggie?"

"There will be no further talk of you taking charge of me," she warned. "I'm *not* your cousin."

"Maggie, I didn't mean it the way it came out," he said softly. "I was trying to protect your reputation. You know me."

"I know nothing about you now, other than you enjoy kissing strange women with little provocation," she complained.

"I argue that point. I was highly provoked by a very tempting woman who enjoyed teasing me. It was not as if you stopped me."

"No, I didn't, did I?" The door rattled as the bolt was drawn back, and Maggie reappeared. She held the door firmly shut against him, though. "Who is Sally Ford?"

"Someone I made up on the spot to torment you with."

"No. I don't think that's true," she said, eyes flashing dangerously. "You were never that good a liar as a boy."

He raked a hand through his hair. Maggie had always seen through him. "All right. I apologize. I kissed Sally Ford some time ago, but I'm sure she'll have forgotten about it by now."

"I imagine that if you kiss everyone like that, few women ever do. Good night, Your Grace."

He put his foot in the door to stop her from shutting it in his face again. "Was the kiss too much?"

A tiny smile tugged her lips. "Too much or too little?" she teased, and then laughed. "Perhaps you'll figure it out by morning. Pleasant dreams, Your Grace."

The door shut, and Algernon sighed, disappointed and oddly challenged by the question.

Maggie had taught him to take nothing for granted when it came to what she wanted. She had changed her mind because of what he'd said to the Keanes downstairs, although he might have presumed too much from her invitation. He ought to have remembered Maggie was not his to order about, though he always tried.

He had overstepped the bounds of propriety well and truly by kissing her like that, too.

Tomorrow, he would ask permission before he kissed her again.

CHAPTER FIVE

THE FIRST COACH from London arrived without warning early the next morning, dropping only two passengers at the inn but confirming the road behind was clear. Excitement surged, and the delayed carriages were prepared in a flurry of activity while travelers gathered outside in the mud, eager to be away.

Maggie joined the line of travelers attempting to board the first coach headed for London the next morning, only to be disappointed when it filled too quickly.

She hugged her travel case close to her chest and shuffled toward the next coach, determined not to have her sole possession wrested from her grip in the confusion and lost forever. She could not afford to lose what little the case contained.

The second carriage was declared ready for boarding quite quickly, and the crowd surged forward. Maggie was swept along with everyone else, desperate not to miss her chance for a seat inside, out of the weather.

She struggled to make headway, only to suddenly be wrenched out of line—lifted off her feet, in fact—and deposited to the side, where it soon became apparent that she would now be the last to board and have to cling to the back of the carriage.

She turned, irritated, and found herself gazing into the equally irritated eyes of the Duke of Ravenswood.

"And where are you going this morning—without saying goodbye, I might add?"

Dear God, Algernon had grown into a bossy devil.

"I am continuing toward London, of course," she said, pointing obviously at the carriage that was now almost full. She wrenched her arm from his. "I might have had a place inside, too, if you had let me go!"

He glanced at the carriage and frowned. "I am not letting you board a carriage like that," he announced. "Not before you give me a chance to talk about yesterday's kiss."

Maggie peered down the empty road, filled with exasperation. "You're regretting that it happened at all, and you're about to beg my forgiveness and swear it will never happen again?"

"I regret nothing, but I will behave if you ask me to."

She glanced at him in surprise, but then shook her head firmly. "Goodbye, Ravenswood."

He caught her arm, preventing her escape.

"Look, there are only two coaches, and the second is nearly full. Who knows when the next one will arrive? I cannot stay here another night just to talk to you."

"I'm not asking you to, but there are other ways for you to get to where you want to go, and in greater speed and comfort, I might add."

"How? Where?"

"The carriage you need is being prepared at the stables as we speak. As soon as these two carriages have departed the front of the inn, you will board it—with *me*."

"With you? Have you lost your mind altogether?"

"Not yet, but I'm still young," he promised with a cheeky grin. "You will find my carriage far more comfortable than any other, I assure you."

"Why would you want me in your carriage?"

"For the same reason you gave me your pillow. Simple kindness. There are still some days of travel before we reach London, and I cannot think of a better way to spend the hours than discussing everything and anything with you, my old friend."

"That is hardly proper," she said, astonished by his offer to share. They were not related. They were not anything to each other but very old acquaintances who had kissed on a dare. Well, a few dares, actually.

"There are many ways to get around the appearance of impropriety, and posing as a member of my vast family is nearly foolproof."

"If I were a member of your family, you'd risk being murdered by me for your high-handed ways," she muttered darkly.

At that, he only laughed. "Well, I am often accused of being high-handed. However, in this case, it is for your benefit. You might consider traveling with me as repayment for sharing your soft pillow with me last night. I did sleep better for it."

She smiled briefly, but her stomach pitted, painfully aware that others were listening. She stepped back from the carriage to consider Algernon's invitation fully.

To travel alone in his carriage was madness. To be seen doing so could ruin her reputation completely. But Algernon was always in a hurry. She could reach her destination so much faster if she traveled with him. To say no would mean enduring lonely days and extra nights at the mercy of innkeepers greedy for her coin.

The innkeeper of the Stag was standing

about outside in the sun, watching his paying customers take their leave, receiving new guests... and then he noticed Maggie. He frowned at her. But when his gaze shifted to the duke, his smile brightened. No doubt he was anticipating he'd get more coin from them both.

Maggie had little money to spare to pay for rooms along the way as it was. She had to continue, but she would much rather travel swiftly in a larger carriage than be crushed. Or rained on, gripping to the back of a mail coach.

But accepting would mean incurring a debt to the duke that could only be repaid when she found Papa.

She worried her lip. The duke's carriage had looked quite large, even broken, and no doubt it was terribly comfortable, now it was fixed.

And there was the added danger—he might want to kiss her again.

Maggie wasn't sure that was a good idea. It had been an age since a gentleman had taken any interest in her, but at least she knew where she stood with a duke. Algernon would never hint at making her an offer of marriage just to get beneath her skirts, if he even thought about it anymore.

She considered her options, but she had none better. A lady's reputation might be ruined during any carriage ride with a bachelor, but it could survive a journey if they claimed to be cousins.

She met Algernon's gaze again, and she could see that he knew she had no other choice by the way he grinned back at her. He had been just like that as a boy, reading her mind, especially when his arguments had won her over. He was doing so again—and far too easily for her comfort.

"As long as no one discovers the lie, I suppose it could not hurt to at least travel with you to the next town," she agreed. "I am not going all the way to London, after all—and I shall not be telling my father about our arrangement, either."

"I should be very happy to take you directly to him."

"No."

Algernon pressed his lips together. "To the town nearest his place of employment it is, then."

That was more acceptable to Maggie. "Very well."

"I'll lend you my book to pass the time," he offered. "But don't berate me for its poor condition. It got a bit damp."

She smiled, overcome by a wave of relief that he was still the generous boy she remembered. Algernon had always shared the things that mattered to her. Books were her favorite things in all the world. That, and her new favorite: his kisses.

"Thank you."

"Think nothing of it." He held out his arm. "Most likely, you have read it already. It's from home. From Ravenswood's library."

"I remember the library," she replied, although she wasn't sure she did. Thanks to her father's many positions as tutor to great families, she'd seen so many that they had all blurred together. The Ravenswood library had undoubtedly been a place of wonder and riches beyond her reach though.

"Well, where is this carriage of yours, cousin?" she said, squaring her shoulders.

"*Our* carriage," the duke corrected, as he held out his arm again. "It is this way, dear cousin."

Maggie blushed at the warmth of his voice and slipped her arm through his—something she had not done with a gentleman in a long time, either, and certainly never with Algernon, who used to put two hands on top of her shoulders and steer her everywhere, especially out of the library to play.

Thinking of those special days made it easier to pretend she was as important as him, though she refused to let him carry her traveling case.

She went with him willingly, picking their way down the muddy street, lifting her skirts high to avoid ruining the hem with mud. But there was no chance of saving her best shoes from utter ruin because when they reached the stable yard, there was a great puddle of soft mud between them and the waiting ducal carriage.

Algernon suddenly swept her up into his arms and, despite her weak protests that she could walk herself there, carried her across the revolting stable yard.

The grooms surrounding the carriage grinned and whispered, and Maggie's face warmed again with an unstoppable blush. "You should not have done that," she complained in a whisper.

"Anyone watching will think that I have a gallant soul, ensuring that my cousin's shoes and skirts remain free of mud and muck," he said loudly, clearly for his men to hear. "Men, allow me to introduce my cousin, Mrs. Black. You will all ensure her journey with us is without incident, and watch your language."

"I would appreciate your restraint," she said to them. "Now put me down, you great lump," she demanded, thumping Algernon's shoulder. "Gentlemen do not hold their cousins for so long."

"Be still, Maggie," he whispered. "We need to make sure the mud stays out of our carriage, too."

One of the men whipped out a rag and wiped any mud carefully off her boots, and then Ravenswood tossed her unceremoniously onto one of the well-padded seats within, before stooping to awkwardly wipe the mud from his own once-glossy black boots.

He took a place at her side and passed over her pillow. "Returned in perfect condition." He smiled and gestured around them. "Surely this is more appealing than the overloaded mail coach, dear cousin."

Maggie glanced around, admiring the blue velvet cushions beneath her bottom, and noting the fine quality of the paneling and the thick velvet draperies at the windows. She was shabby by comparison. "Yes, I suppose this is tolerable," she replied, as haughtily as she could manage.

That earned her a laugh from Algernon, and he called up to the coachman that they could depart at his convenience.

Maggie set her travel case at her feet against the wall, as another man joined them inside. The fellow sat opposite the duke on the rear-facing seat and, after setting down a wicker basket, smiled hesitantly at her.

Algernon sighed. "This is my valet, Sims. Our chaperone. Sims, this is Maggie Black. She visited Ravenswood before your time. Please refer to her as my married cousin at all future stops."

"Mrs. Black," he said, following the duke's instructions.

"Mr. Sims," she replied, a little discomfited

by the lie of being a married woman, even if she agreed it was a good idea.

"Maggie, if you require anything along the way, just ask him or me," Algernon said, reaching for the case the valet had brought with him and opening it.

"I do apologize for your employer's insistence that I accompany you," she said to Sims.

The fellow grinned. "There is no stopping a duke when he wants what he wants."

"Yes, I do recall that bad habit of his from childhood," she murmured.

"I'm sure everyone complains about it at some point, too," the valet agreed with a soft laugh.

While a servant probably should not have made fun of his employer, Maggie could tell that the fellow held Algernon in great affection, and indeed, the reverse seemed true as well, because Algernon did not chide Sims for the impertinent remark.

Sims pulled out a slim volume and a lead pencil from within his coat and listened to the duke while making some quick notes inside the pages, before putting it away again. The pair spoke of the road ahead and some other business matters as they got underway, and then the valet was given leave to amuse himself.

Algernon, once the carriage started to gain

speed, braced himself with one foot across the door, the other knee edged toward her, leaving Maggie still with a good amount of space on the right side of the carriage. She appreciated the leg room after yesterday's cramped journey, squashed between her fellow travelers and the leaking door.

Algernon sighed loudly as they passed the next river crossing without incident. "I never thought we would win free."

"You make it sound like you were held prisoner there," Maggie noted. "It was not a bad place."

"Did you eat dinner at all last night? I recall a certain young girl as little impressed with stew as I have always been."

She smiled slightly, having enjoyed the evening meal last night simply because someone else had done the cooking. "I am sorry dinner was not to your liking, Your Grace. Perhaps if you used your title, the service and quality offered at inns would improve."

"Your company last night would have made up for any disappointment in the meal," he promised. "The private dining room did feel rather full—and certainly I had no friend by my side to entertain me."

"A pity you could not carry a book in to dinner. But people tend to find it rude when you read at the dining table," she noted.

"I can't imagine why," Algernon said, but his grin suggested otherwise.

"The second-to-next town should provide an opportunity to purchase books, Your Grace," the valet promised.

"Well, there you have it. Sims will find books for us both after we have eaten luncheon," Algernon announced, glancing down at the wicker basket at their feet.

"Sims does not have to purchase anything for me," she said. But Algernon's glance at the picnic basket and mention of luncheon made her stomach rumble in anticipation of their next stop.

Thankfully, no one heard.

"It would be my pleasure to be of assistance, Mrs. Black. It is part of my duties to keep the duke amused at all times," Sims confessed, with another smirk for his employer. "And every member of his family, too."

"Indeed, it is his job," Ravenswood agreed. "And if Mrs. Black is happy, then I shall surely be too, though perhaps she would like to choose her own books?"

"An excellent idea, Your Grace," Sims answered. The valet settled back with his head against the squabs, smiling, and closed his eyes.

Within a few minutes, the fellow seemed to be sleeping.

Maggie leaned toward the duke, raising a brow and glancing at the valet. "I can never sleep traveling backward."

"It is a skill," he said. "Sims is available to me day and night, so he catches his sleep when he can, and I never complain about his lack of conversation. He's an exceptional servant."

"It must be nice to have someone to look after you all the time," she said, more than a little envious. Maggie hadn't had a lady's maid in years, or a housekeeper in months. She could not afford the expense of more than occasional maid service.

"Indeed, it is," he said. His gaze lowered to her lips, and he licked his own. "Sims and the men will say nothing about you traveling with me, I promise. They will be the soul of discretion."

Maggie bit her lip, too, imagining Algernon's lips pressed against hers again. The man had been delicious, and more experienced and exciting than her one and only beau had ever been. But they were not alone in the carriage now, and she looked away from the temptation he presented. "I'm glad, because I would not like to cause trouble for you."

"You have never been trouble for me, Maggie,

but I would not like to anger your father and have to meet him on the field of honor."

Maggie winced. "I wouldn't like that, either, when there is no reason for him to doubt your character."

Father already believed the worst of *her*, and there was nothing she could do about that now.

Algernon suddenly fussed around with his own travel case. He offered her a book. "As promised."

She took the book, flicked through the damp pages, and smirked. "Were you reading this when you fell out of the carriage door?"

The duke's eyes widened. "How did you know I fell out..."

Maggie laughed.

"Oh, I ought to put you over my knee for tricking me into admitting to that. You rob me of my dignity so easily."

"I cannot help it if you are so easy to tease, Your Grace." She flicked through to the end of the book.

"You never used to read that fast," Algernon complained, when she closed the volume.

"I have read this before," she admitted, but opened the book again. "No matter. I will enjoy it again if we read it together."

He nodded and produced a pair of spectacles.

"So the Duke of Ravenswood is not immune to old age, either?" she murmured, producing her own.

"So it seems." Algernon grinned but put his glasses away again. "You know, I have not had the pleasure of listening to your voice these past years. I have missed you dearly."

A small blush heated her cheeks, and she struggled to contain her pleasure at hearing such an unexpected compliment from him. Usually, most people disliked her habit of reading out loud and claimed it was a detriment to her character, not something to miss.

Maggie began on the first page, and continued to read to her captive audience as the day rolled on. She turned page after page, her voice steady, pretending not to notice the way Algernon watched her lips so closely—like a man captivated by what he sees.

CHAPTER SIX

"I TOLD you that we would pass the stage," Algernon crowed, nudging her arm so she would lift her head from her book.

Maggie sighed loudly and turned the page. "Yes, you did. As always, the Duke of Ravenswood is correct."

Algernon frowned at her. He did not like this new habit of Maggie's—calling him by his title. But he couldn't seem to insist that she should not do it. Of course, she argued that a family member would only call him by his title, and that such a respectful manner of address was no less than he deserved.

And yet, this was Maggie.

Maggie, who had bested him in mathematics more times than he could count. Maggie, whose knowledge of history at ten had been something terrifying to behold. Maggie, who had challenged him and refused to pretend she wasn't smarter. And likely, she still was, though she was much better at hiding it now.

They had spent much of the day taking turns to read the book out loud, but eventually he had tired of it. Maggie had read in silence after that and looked to be near the end, thank God. Although whenever she stopped reading, she would, of course, question his insistence that she travel in the comfort of his carriage beyond the next town they'd agreed upon. Insisting she ought to take the mail coach, as she had originally intended to do.

But if she were on the mail coach, and he remained in his carriage alone, he would not be able to talk with her. And he was enjoying that—renewing their acquaintance, catching up on the events of her life, and telling her about the antics of his younger brothers and wider family.

From the little Maggie had revealed about her *own* life, he was concerned about her father's disappearance, too, as it did not seem rational. His correspondence to his daughter had always been a constant factor during their estrangement. His old tutor took up a new position every other year, moving from student to student as they outgrew his tutelage.

Algernon had outgrown Mr. Black's teaching quite quickly, long before the year was up. However, he had not outgrown Maggie's. Their conversations outside of the classroom, between lessons, had challenged him to expand his education in ways he hadn't considered possible—nor the way her father had ever suggested, either.

Maggie closed the book and glanced out the window with a sigh. "How much farther?"

"I saw a one-mile marker for a town a few minutes ago," he promised.

"Good. I need to stretch my legs. And I wonder if this place might happen to have that bookseller your valet mentioned."

"We will have to wait and see," he said, glad that he'd decided to stop earlier than planned that day.

"Yes," she said slowly.

He pointed to the book she'd not been reading. One of her own that was sitting on the top of her well-worn travel case. "May I see that?"

She handed it over, and he studied the front. "I don't think I've read this one."

"No?"

"No."

"Well, it's yours now, a small repayment for all your help. Read it at your leisure."

They were still some distance away from London due to the slow speed they were traveling, so he gladly accepted the volume, but not as a repayment or with a mind toward keeping it forever. Maggie seemed to have very little with her. She'd worn the same dress for three days in a row.

"I have other books that I can share from my trunk when we stop next—if you would enjoy reading about farming practices and the husbandry of sheep, that is."

She laughed. "Well, that would be a change for me. My last subject was just a bit dry."

"Yes. The temples of faraway countries, as told by an avid explorer," he read from the spine. "Written by a pretentious gentleman of means, I assume?"

"Yes. I long for the day when I find a book written by a woman traveling with limited funds," she said. "So many tellings of travels are dry and without essential details a woman needs. Details of life on the road. Costs. Have you traveled?" she asked, glancing his way.

"Unfortunately, my travels have amounted to trips to London and various estates dotted about the English countryside. If I've gone anywhere, it has only been through the pages of books like this," he admitted. He tucked it beside him to read later, then resumed his study of Maggie. "And you? You always talked of going off to explore the world."

"The dreams of a naïve child. I am well satisfied with my life so far and accept the limitations of it," she claimed.

Algernon did not quite believe her. "And what limitations would those be?"

"Well, the usual—I'm a woman. Women do not set off on many grand adventures, do they? They stay home and tend a house."

"So you have a house to manage," he said, carefully. Maggie had been slow in offering up many personal details of her life so far, especially where she had come from.

"A cottage. Nothing like Ravenswood. My parents had a nice home once, though, and Papa would return there between his teaching engagements for a little while. But then Mama died, and he sold it. I lost count of how many homes I stayed in after that. So when I was twenty, I announced that I would not continue with him anymore."

"Oh? What led to your decision?"

"The usual problem," she said.

Algernon frowned, unsure of what that meant, but by the look in her eyes, it was an unpleasant thing and probably involved some scoundrel disappointing her. Was that why she had not married?

"So you made your own life, friends, and neighbors six years ago?" he queried, deciding it prudent not to press her for details of whatever had happened to her just yet.

"I have few acquaintances, although they

likely would have disapproved of my search for my father, had I told them of my intentions."

"They must be worried about your absence?"

"I suppose they could be, in their own way. There's no one else to read their correspondence for them with me gone. It's really the only place I know now. Everywhere else I've lived is just a vague memory."

"Even Ravenswood?" he asked.

"I remember some of it. The mahogany staircase and you screaming blue murder are clearest."

"That's probably because Stratford kept riding the banister down to the entrance hall. He was five. I was always running after him, trying to catch him before he broke his neck. I remember you there very well," he admitted. "You had a small chamber of your own in the attic, and you were always sitting at the windows, reading instead of coming out to play."

"Well, that is what young ladies of tutors are expected to do when there are no other girls to play with. Be quiet. Don't draw attention to myself. Don't forget my father's position depends on making a good impression with everyone. My father expected me to behave," she reminded him. "You're a fine one to talk, though. You often sat out in the garden against a tree, your nose stuck in a book, too, ignoring your brothers pushing and shoving each other around."

He grinned. "You eventually came out to sit beside me and learned to ignore my brothers as well."

"I never really understood their games, to be honest. At that age, it all seemed so silly trying to wrestle each other to the ground."

He laughed. "Yes, well, they had boundless energy. As the eldest, I was responsible for them. I had to invent excuses to make my brothers run around so that when it was time for their lessons or lectures, they would sit still for them."

"You, however, did not need any urging to sit still for lessons or lectures?"

"I think I did, especially if the tutor was inferior to what I expected. I had one tutor who tried to assure me that it was possible to sail across the ocean and fall off the edge of the world."

"Good grief," she said. "Wasn't that theory disproved long ago?"

"Well, clearly he missed that announcement." He drew closer. "And what of you? Did you ever try your hand at teaching?"

"Goodness, no. My father would never have permitted me to have an occupation."

Algernon studied her. "And even in his absence, you have not tried?"

"I have tried to help my neighbors when they

get their letters, but that is the extent of my tutoring, if you could call it such."

"Oh, that's a shame. You would have made a great teacher, I think, had you been permitted. You were very patient with me."

"I could have been a lot of great things, had I not been born a woman," she grumbled. "Ah, here we are. This looks like a good-sized town ahead."

The village was a thriving little market town. Algernon alighted from the carriage, leaving Maggie inside, and spoke to the valet, who'd been riding the back all afternoon. "Arrange for two rooms—adjoining, if you please, Sims. My cousin is weary."

The valet, knowing Maggie was no relation of his at all, raised a brow in surprise at the request for adjoining rooms, but rushed off to do his bidding without asking questions. Algernon probably shouldn't want an adjoining room, but he'd never enjoyed a conversation more than he had on his journey with Maggie so far. He sensed that there was a great deal Maggie had been denied in her life. It pained him to think of such great intelligence going to waste in a small village where her father had left her, forgotten and underappreciated.

The valet returned and assured him that adjoining rooms were possible. He opened the carriage door to help Maggie out.

The innkeeper rushed toward them. "Sir! A pleasure to see you again—and this time with a wife, no less. Congratulations."

Algernon gaped at the man, while Maggie gasped in obvious shock. "Oh, yes. Um, what did you say?"

"I feared this day would never come," the innkeeper confided, shaking Algernon's hand while beaming at Maggie. "Welcome. I hope you and your husband enjoy your stay at our humble establishment."

"Well, um. Come along, my dear," Algernon held out his hand to Maggie. "I'm sure you need the quiet to recover from our journey."

Maggie turned to look at him pointedly. The longer she studied him, the more hostile her expression became. Eventually, she set her hand in his. "Yes, I think that is a very good idea. I should like some privacy before our next discussion."

Algernon gulped. Oh dear God. This was a disaster.

He escorted her inside the inn and immediately upstairs to the chambers the innkeeper directed them to, his blood pumping wildly in his veins. Married? To Maggie? She was going to ring a peal over his head or kill him. She'd already threatened to do so.

The entire way up the stairs, Maggie's fingertips dug into the back of his hand. He would apologize profusely once they were alone, but the damage was already done to her good opinion of him. He had entirely forgotten that he was known here.

He opened the door for her and allowed her to precede him into the first bedchamber. But before he could cross the threshold to talk, Maggie slammed the door in his face.

He sighed. Yes. That was one imposition too far.

He went to his own chamber and entered a tidy little room. He glanced at the connecting door and went there to knock.

Maggie flung it open. "What were you thinking to ask for a connecting room when you are known here?"

"Yes, I had forgotten about that," he said, as he peeked into her room, noticing it was larger and prettier than his. He approved of that. "I am sorry."

"He will remember meeting your *new wife*, too, the next time you visit," Maggie whispered, clearly horrified.

"Possibly."

"Algernon!" Her eyes narrowed dangerously. "I cannot be your wife."

"I know that. You know that."

She set her hands on her hips. "Why does this not bother you more?"

"I will regret it if he gossips, but I would not change anything about this day."

"You have become reckless. Impulsive. Presumptuous and—"

Algernon quickly put his finger over her lips. "I assure you, I have no intention of bothering you as a real husband might hope to."

He dragged his finger off her lips slowly, and heard a small gasp leave her throat.

Algernon stilled, struck by what he was doing...and wanted to do next most of all: find any excuse to kiss her again.

He *was* being reckless, and normally would act on his impulses around a woman he fancied. But Maggie was his dear friend, and he ought to behave with more restraint around her until invited to do otherwise. She had not voiced such an invitation yet, though there had been ample glances that suggested she was considering his appeal.

He stepped back from her. "Have dinner in your chamber if you wish to punish me for wanting you near, Maggie. I deserve it."

He pivoted and retraced his steps to the door, deciding that Maggie might need time to cool her temper before she would forgive him.

The inn boasted a taproom, and he went

there to wait at a table near a window. The ale was decent and the room warm, and he drowsed a little as the room filled with newcomers, and considered what he was doing with Maggie.

Maggie, while highly desirable, was the last woman an indebted duke should flirt with so often. She had said little about her circumstances, but he'd gleaned enough to piece together that she lived in near poverty and was disappointed with her life. Her cloak hid from most the poor condition of her gown, but the soles of her shoes were nearly worn through.

He could not be another disappointment to her.

And yet he had thought all day of kissing her again. Today, and since meeting Maggie again, he had ignored that he was traveling to London to rendezvous with a wealthy viscountess.

Lady Stephanie Kent had the connections, the pedigree, and the elegance, not to mention the money, to provide Algernon's immediate needs in a bride.

But the idea of marrying her did not appeal. Not when there was no affection between them. He had tried to like her more last season, and failed. He hoped further time spent with the woman before he proposed might rectify that situation. And it was why he was headed to London...to see her again and find the right moment to propose.

Algernon was sipping his fifth tankard when he heard a shrill laugh that reminded him of Lady Kent. He repressed a shiver, which was not the correct reaction for a prospective groom to have at all.

When he heard the piercing noise again, he sat up straighter and glanced around the taproom.

A hush had settled over the taproom patrons in the hour he'd been there, and the laugh came from no one nearby. He turned his eyes to the open window and spied a carriage he recognized standing directly outside the inn.

The distinctive black and blue wavy stripe along the side of Lady Kent's carriage was unmistakable.

He blinked in surprise to see her here...but she was not alone.

Lady Stephanie Kent and a strange man appeared to be grappling inside her carriage—mid-tryst.

Algernon narrowed his eyes at her brazen behavior. It was one thing for a widow to rendezvous with a lover in a carriage after dark, but another to do it in broad daylight with the carriage blinds tied back.

The fellow struggled to escape through the

open door, held in place by Lady Kent as they exchanged heated kisses. As soon as the fellow's feet hit the ground, though, he stumbled back and she was driven off with a regal wave.

Algernon watched the fellow rush into the taproom and survey those inside, while straightening his hair and tugging down his sensible brown waistcoat.

The man was utterly unremarkable in appearance. Sandy-brown hair, sensibly attired and not obviously wealthy.

But he was younger than Algernon by a half-dozen years.

The man requested a tankard of ale and headed toward the only vacant chair in the room.

The one opposite Algernon.

"Do you mind if I join you, sir?" he asked. His voice was soft, hesitant. Timid almost.

"No, not at all," Algernon murmured, made uncomfortable by the request, but curiosity won out. Who was Lady Kent's new lover?

After a moment, he met Algernon's gaze. "Are you a local, sir?"

"No. Just passing through," he promised, relieved not to be recognized. "And you?"

"Yes. Passing through as well." The fellow glanced around. "But I was hoping someone knew of a position I could apply for."

"I've no knowledge of one," Algernon answered, struck by the oddity of the question. Algernon hadn't heard a whisper about Lady Kent engaged in any affairs before today. "Are you in search of a position?"

"Not exactly," the fellow said, turning red.

Algernon fell silent as he sipped his tankard, considering what to say next to the man. But as he watched the young man ignore his own drink, he revised his assumptions. The fellow couldn't be more than twenty, perhaps even younger than that. He still had spots! What was Lady Kent doing, kissing a mere boy?

Algernon sat forward. "Where are you headed?"

"To London."

Lady Kent's carriage had been pointed in the opposite direction from London. Had she taken a journey solely to seduce her young lover? He tried to remember if she owned property nearby, but he did not think so.

"Do you live in London?"

"I'm a... Yes."

Algernon thought about the way he answered. The fellow had just held his tongue over a longer explanation. The boy was a *servant*.

Algernon glanced out the window again to hide his shock. *Lady Kent's* servant, it seemed. The boy was new to her employ, if that was so.

"London is a place of great opportunity for ambitious young men."

"I thought so, too. Until..."

Algernon sat back. "Until?"

"Nothing," the fellow hedged, looking around guiltily. As he turned his head, Algernon noticed small bite marks on his throat.

Algernon's skin prickled with distaste. "Are you in any difficulty, sir?"

"No, of course not," the fellow whispered, though he sounded horrified by the question.

Dear God, he was just a boy and out of his depth.

Algernon struggled to keep the revulsion off his face for what Lady Kent might have done with him, and not just in her carriage. He'd seen this before, but usually it was a young maid imposed upon by a male employer, not a footman or groom unwillingly seduced by the lady of the house. They fell silent for a while as Algernon considered what he should do or could say to the young man. Getting involved with an employer, was not bound to help him succeed in the end. He finished his ale, watching the young man sip and hide a grimace at the taste his own. All the young man sank deeper into his chair.

After twenty minutes of silence, Algernon tapped his finger to get his attention. "Were you serious about finding new employment?"

"No. Not really." The fellow quickly ran a hand through his hair, discreetly checking his clothing, too. "It was just an idle fancy of mine to seek a more challenging position."

Algernon's curiosity was utterly piqued now.

The fellow glanced out the window, suddenly grew pale, and shrank down in his chair so he could not be seen easily. He buried his nose in his tankard again.

Algernon glanced outside, too, and spied Lady Kent's carriage standing directly out front of the inn again. He did not bother to hide himself when the lady he had intended to marry returned for her young lover.

Eventually, the young man sighed and stood up. Clearly, he thought he had no choice but to continue to please Lady Kent.

"A pleasant day to you, sir," he mumbled, sounding defeated.

"One moment," Algernon murmured. "I tend to trust my instincts, and if I were you, I would seek a new position sooner rather than later."

The fellow agreed and headed for the door. Algernon stood up and then turned to go upstairs to his chambers, deep in thought. How often did Lady Kent engage in affairs with her servants? He would have to look into that before he proposed.

He let himself into his chamber, needing to

be alone with his troubling discovery. He would have to confront her about his suspicions. If he found further evidence of such dalliances, he could not marry a woman prone to sleeping with just anyone. He required his heir to be his own offspring, and for there to be no doubts in his mind about that.

Suddenly, Maggie was rushing toward him. "Where have you been? I was worried sick about you!"

"Only in the taproom," he said, blinking in surprise at her complaint. He captured her hands when she drew close enough, humbled by her concern.

She had worried for him? Of all the people in the world, it was Maggie who missed him, and that touched him deeply.

He kissed the back of her hands, and then tucked a strand of hair behind her ear. "There was no reason to be worried."

"I thought you had abandoned me. We've only just married," she complained.

Algernon started to apologize—and then re-membered they were not married at all. He laughed, understanding that he'd been forgiven in his absence, and for the pretense of being a married couple. Her teasing was good for him. She turned his mind from his problems so easily.

Even as children, Maggie had always tried to soothe him.

It was a quality he desired in a wife.

Maggie stared up at him, and then her smile slowly slipped away. "Something happened while we were apart. What?"

She could read his moods, too.

So he told her about meeting the young man in the taproom, and his obvious reluctance to return to his employer's carriage, along with his suspicions of a scandalous affair taking place.

But he kept back that he was on his way to meet the same woman with a view to making her his wife.

"It does sound suspicious, indeed. I do hope the young man takes your advice and finds a new position soon," she murmured.

CHAPTER SEVEN

WHEN ALGERNON INTRODUCED Maggie as *Mrs. Black* and himself as *Mr. Black* the next day at dinner, Maggie bit back a groan that the ruse would continue, albeit under a lesser description. As a boy, Algernon had been almost embarrassed by his title, yet for some reason, he seemed to relish this ruse of being her devoted husband.

As she sat by his side, she tried to imagine what it might be like to be his wife in truth. Never a dull moment. Never left out of conversations. Her opinions sought and valued.

It was soothing after fending for herself for so long.

She patted her lips, full to the brim of another fine and expensive dinner she couldn't afford herself, and turned to Algernon, keen to hear more about his life and family. "And your youngest brother? Is he still painting the walls in the attics?"

"Stratford? No, he moved on to actual canvas years ago, and he can now paint quite openly with my father gone."

The woman across from them at the dining table leaned forward. "Oh? Was there something scandalous about his paintings, sir?"

A flicker of annoyance crossed Algernon's face, but he answered her. "My father disapproved of the arts, and for some time, my brother practiced in secret," he explained. "My father refused to let his sons engage in what he thought of as useless occupations or something they might enjoy."

"It is a great skill to be able to draw and paint with ease," Maggie murmured.

"Yes, I quite agree. My siblings are free now to do as they please, without criticism from anyone."

"You are a very good brother," the lady opposite suggested, batting her lashes at Algernon right in front of Maggie.

The woman was beginning to annoy her. The widow kept cutting into their conversation and flirting with Algernon, when she wasn't bemoaning her solitary state.

She leaned forward a little, fiddling with the neckline of her gown as she gazed at Algernon with barely hidden interest. "Gentlemen like you must surely be appreciated by any woman, especially his wife."

Maggie stifled a sigh. It was only the third time the woman had subtly questioned whether Algernon was happily married, but it was not out of hope for conjugal bliss for *them*. She clearly hoped Algernon was unhappy with his choice.

But Algernon smiled and reached for Maggie's hand, gripping it tightly. "I am indeed the luckiest of men to have captured this clever, beautiful woman for my wife. I don't know how she puts up with me."

Maggie lowered her chin to hide her embarrassment at Algernon's statement. His lies were getting out of hand.

"Oh, well. That's wonderful to hear," the woman promised, fluttering her fan furiously.

"Yes, I tell our children that they should hope for a love like ours every day of their lives," Algernon continued, lifting Maggie's hand to kiss her fingers and smiling like he was besotted. "And of course, to adore their dear mama as much as I do."

Maggie lifted her head to stare at Algernon. *In love, married for two days, and they already had children?*

Algernon's expression was one of devilry, because he could say what he liked in front of others and Maggie couldn't really stop him.

She shook her head, resigned to more foolishness to come out of his mouth the longer they lingered at the table. He was Mr. Black, not the Duke of Ravenswood, or even Algernon Sweet. His ruse continued to break all the rules of polite society and was only getting worse the longer they were together.

"I hope you know how lucky you are," the lady said to Maggie.

"I tell her that all the time," Algernon promised. "But I couldn't do without her now, either."

Eventually, the woman nodded, her expression envious and conceding defeat to Maggie's claim on her handsome husband. She bid them good night and moved away, but stopped to speak with another, less-attractive man. Though she looked back at Algernon a few times, clearly regretting what could never be.

Maggie turned to the duke. "How many children do we have?"

"Two at least."

"I see," Maggie murmured. "An heir and a spare, I assume."

"One of each sex," he announced firmly. "At least that is my hope."

"I was afraid you'd want at least four, like your papa."

"I'm not like him."

"I'm glad you are not," she promised.

Maggie had encountered the old duke, Algernon's father, several times during her stay at Ravenswood. Heard him belittle and criticize his sons and try to tell her father how Algernon should be punished for his mistakes.

Algernon had been one of her father's best and brightest students without needing an incentive. He was dedicated to his studies and inquisitive, and most definitely had always wanted to come first.

Maggie had bested him often. On the odd occasion when she was feeling extremely uncharitable, she let her true intelligence show and finished well before he could make it halfway through a test.

However, that had not met with her father's approval, and as a consequence, she had been banished from his classroom in the end, and after departing Ravenswood, she had tried to hide that side of herself from his later pupils.

When anyone discovered that she had a brain as well as a little beauty, she would either be taunted for being a bluestocking or pursued to prove she was weaker than her pursuer in some other way. Maggie could handle the name-calling. She'd learned that some boys felt threatened by a girl of greater intelligence. But the cruel attempts at seduction for the sake of their egos were something she could live without experiencing again.

Algernon had not been like that as a boy. He'd been surprised that she was smarter than he had expected her to be, but never behaved as if he'd felt threatened by that fact. He'd befriended her instead.

"And you have sisters-in-law, too? Now, that must be quite the novelty, having women constantly underfoot and running your home."

He laughed. "My sisters are a delight, and I think they will like you very much."

She laughed again. "It is unlikely our paths will ever cross."

"I should be very happy to invite you to stay with us again," he promised.

"I'm sure my father would be pleased to be received by the esteemed Duke of Ravenswood," she told him quietly. She pushed her plate aside and stood. "I believe I will turn in for the night. Good evening, everyone."

In a moment, Algernon was on his feet as well. He caught her hand and kissed the back of it. "Good night, Mrs. Black. I will join you soon."

He probably said as much because the other

guests were listening—and because the widow's eyes had lit up with anticipation.

Maggie left the dining room and trudged back up the stairs, noticing that the rain had eased off again. There had been lightning about in the afternoon, forcing Algernon to call a halt to their journey earlier than expected that day.

But perhaps tomorrow they could leave early, and the roads would be dry enough that they could make up for lost time.

Once in her room, Maggie removed her shawl and gloves and set them aside. She was tired and eager for sleep. But just as she was considering undressing, a tentative knock sounded on the door that connected to Algernon's chamber.

When she opened it, she found him on the other side, grinning. "God, that woman couldn't give us a moment of peace."

"She fancied you," Maggie warned him, hugging the door. "Did you arrange an assignation for later?"

"I did not fancy *her*," he protested. "Are you going to invite me in tonight or hand me another pillow?"

Questions like that were how reputations unraveled—one indulgent moment at a time.

But they were already pretending to be married, so technically, she was already ruined.

She stepped back, allowing him entry to her

room, although she knew she really should maintain some separation. She was unmarried, and Algernon was definitely not her husband or likely to be. If they were found to be living a lie, her reputation would be in tatters. Yet, she was enjoying her private conversations with a man so far above her that she didn't want to stop. He made her laugh. His grin was always so warm and infectious that she couldn't help but look forward to the next outrageous thing he might say.

"Ah." He looked around, hands on his hips. "A duke would normally be given the best room at the inn, but I see they gave it to you instead."

She smiled. "I suppose I could trade with you, but I don't want to."

He laughed as his eyes fell on the settee near the fire. "I could almost fit on that, though," he said, going over and trying it out for size. "We could talk all night like we used to do."

"You're welcome to take the settee to your room, if you can carry it through the door on your own," she offered.

"I could, but then you'd have to come to my room and sleep in my bed." He glanced her way with a question in his eyes.

"No," she told him, hiding how the question tempted her to agree.

"Well then, we shall have to make do with

what we've been given. We can talk through the open door."

She laughed. "Poor Algernon, reduced to the indignity of having to raise his voice just to be heard."

"And I invite you to do the same."

Maggie shook her head. "I can't shout at you, Your Grace."

"Why not? My family all do."

"Well, that's different, you know—you and I are not related. We did not grow up together."

"We spent a year together, Maggie. Just one precious year, and you left an indelible mark on my life. You fired all my rebellions against my father's tyranny and prejudices. He learned his lesson after that year, though. My father never allowed anyone to have such influence or access to me again."

She looked at him in surprise. "Did you have no other teachers after Father?"

"Yes, I did. But none as good as him. And no one challenged me the way you ever did that one year."

"I'm glad I could be of some help with your education. But I'm sure you did not miss me as much as you claim."

"I'm overjoyed to have found you again, Maggie." He sat on her settee and patted the space beside him. "Come, we still have years to catch up on and little time."

She stared at the spot beside him. It would be foolish. Improper. Dangerous. And the temptation to know him better was utterly irresistible.

Maggie settled in the space beside him and sighed. "I missed you, as well."

"I'm glad," Algernon whispered, and then raked a hand through his hair. "I ran after you."

"What? When?"

Algernon sighed heavily. "I was so upset to learn you had been taken away from Ravenswood without us having a chance to say goodbye that I sprinted up the drive in the hope of catching your carriage," he admitted.

"The first I knew of us leaving was when I was woken up that morning before dawn. Papa was already packed. I think something must have happened between your father and mine the evening before," she admitted. "He was cross with me."

"Knowing my father's temper, I suspect they had always disagreed about something or another. The last straw seemed to be my dunking in the muddy pond when I should have been still at my studies."

"It was not that you should have been studying. I laughed when I saw the state you were in. We were kicked off the estate the next day," she suggested. "A whole month before my father's tenure should have ended."

"But you always laughed at me."

"But it was the first time I forgot myself and laughed at you in front of your father. I have felt bad about that ever since."

Algernon covered her hand with his and their fingers entwined. "Don't. I did a great many silly things on purpose just to make you laugh. You could be so serious at times."

Maggie tightened her grip on his fingers. "I still am."

"I was also trying to win you over," he admitted. "I wanted you to like *me* more than our library."

"Both won me on the first day. You told me that I could read any book I wanted," she said, grinning. "I've never forgotten that kindness."

Algernon raised her hand to his lips and kissed her fingers.

The sweet gesture made her pulse speed up as she stared at his lips for too long. She gulped and lowered her eyes, tugging her fingers back. When she looked up, Algernon was watching her still.

Maggie stared at him and felt a shift in his regard. He was not thinking of her as that little girl, but as a woman he fancied.

They moved toward each other at the same time.

Maggie wrapped her arms about Algernon's neck and kissed him. She'd been hoping he might make the first move, but there had been servants around them all day.

Now they were alone, there was nothing to keep them apart. She wanted more of his kisses, and Algernon seemed only too happy to supply.

She found herself under him all too soon, but then Algernon sighed against her throat and became still. "Maggie, what happened between you and your father?"

She was taken aback by the question, which had come out of nowhere, and it poured cold water over her passion. She had not wanted to discuss her scandal with him. He might feel she deserved the ill will that came her way.

He rose up on one elbow, slipped his fingers under her chin, and drew her eyes to his. "What was the cause of your separation?"

Maggie blushed. "This."

"This?" he repeated, frowning.

"Back then, I thought I was in love. I thought I was being courted." She sighed and sat up, straightening her gown. "He was one of my father's students."

Algernon sat up, too. "You were seduced?"

"He almost succeeded, yes."

Algernon shifted to sit close by her side and took up her hand. "Tell me everything."

Maggie rubbed her brow. "He was a year younger than I, and I thought he truly liked me. I thought we were good friends. I thought his interest was genuine. Until the day I heard him complaining about me following him around to his brothers. So I stopped talking to him. I kept to my room and tried to avoid him."

"Good."

"But he didn't like being ignored."

Algernon's arm wrapped about her back, and she leaned into his touch. "Did he hurt you?"

"He broke my heart," she whispered. "He made it seem to others that I was obsessed with him. I found his things hidden in my room. Things I'd never touched or seen before. He would wait for me on the staircases, pull me close, and then push me away just as a servant came along. He made it seem like I was pursuing *him*, that I was promiscuous. Eventually, the whispers reached my father's ears."

"What did he do?"

"Outwardly, nothing until his tenure ended."

"And after?"

"A lecture for me and then silence for a week. He could barely look at me. He believed I had shamed him and ruined myself. He believed what he'd heard from others before he listened to his own daughter. I still possessed my virtue but he called me a liar." She burst to her feet. "My father could not imagine that one of his precious students might attempt to seduce his blue-stocking daughter without some sort of encouragement. I must have been the one who'd crossed a line."

Algernon was suddenly behind her, pulling her into his arms again. "You believed him sincerely interested in you."

"I did." Maggie patted Algernon's arms and stepped away from him. "He never had any real intentions toward me, just saw me as a challenge to conquer. In the end, he wanted to put me in my place. To beat me in the only way he knew how. Proving the weakness of my sex." Maggie drew in a great shuddering breath and let it out slowly. "But it was a long time ago, and I learned my lesson after that. Men are not to be trusted."

Algernon shuffled his feet, clearly uncomfortable with her statement.

She went to him and patted his chest. "*You*, I do trust."

"Why am I trusted and other men are not?" he asked, frowning. He glanced at the settee beside them. "Especially after all that we have done."

"Because you are Algernon, Duke of Ravenswood," she said. "I welcome your kisses and affection, but know you would never marry someone like me. I will not be misled, should anything occur between us. And anything that does will always be my decision. Not because you force me into your arms, but because I want to be there."

Algernon nodded. "As it should always be between us."

"I'm glad you understand," Maggie said, looking around. "I don't expect permanence anymore, or wedding bells, either. Respect is all I hope for."

Algernon looked ready to protest, but she pressed her finger over his lips.

"Let's not talk about our affair any longer. Let's talk about something more important," Maggie said as she sat down on the settee again and patted the space beside her. "Tell me more about Ravenswood. I want to hear all the changes you have planned for the next five years."

He sat beside her, though a little farther away than the last time. "How do you know I have plans that far ahead?"

Maggie laughed softly. "Algernon, whenever have you not had some far-reaching scheme in mind?"

"You know me too well, Maggie Black," he murmured, and began to explain his plans for the site where the maze currently stood.

CHAPTER EIGHT

ALGERNON LAUGHED OUT LOUD. "I just remembered our foot races all those years ago, and the dirty tricks you used to get past Jasper so you wouldn't come last."

Maggie shrugged, but her cheeks turned red, a sure sign she was embarrassed. "The actions of a child should not be held against them as an adult."

"It was an inspired strategy." He laughed at her embarrassment that was hardly called for. Maggie had cried out as if in pain, and Jasper had stopped, concerned for her well-being, only to have Maggie sprint past him to take third place. "Jasper sulked the rest of the day, even though it was a trick he frequently used on Stratford to make *him* come last."

"So I had noticed," Maggie confessed, and then laughed. "I promised Stratford that I would eventually beat Jasper for him one day. I never break my promises."

It had been another wonderful day, full of fond reminiscences and camaraderie—something he hadn't experienced with someone other than a brother in a very long time. Maggie did not care that he was titled. Except for the odd teasing mention of being a duke now, she didn't bow and scrape like others seemed to find necessary. She was entirely herself with him, and Algernon appreciated that after the revelations of the day before.

She was not to blame for the actions of a spoiled, privileged young man who believed he deserved to have Maggie, no matter her opinion on the subject. She had done nothing wrong, and her father should have defended her. Believed in her good character, like Algernon always had.

"Ravenswood had never seen the like until recently. My brothers' wives remind me of you, by the way. Fiercely competitive in their own ways. All stubborn, inventive, and uncommonly pretty. They spin my brothers' heads like nursery tops."

"Well, that is for the best. The right wife can keep her husband well-grounded."

The carriage began to slow, and Algernon looked ahead, spotting the rooflines and chimneys of a village. The sight disappointed him, and he made a spur-of-the-moment decision. They would stop here for the night, even though continuing would not tax the horses' strength unduly to reach London before nightfall.

However, the urgency of a journey that had weighed upon him when he'd first started out had dissipated entirely.

He was having too much fun with Maggie—a situation that would likely never come his way again. She had termed their time together as an affair, and he did not disagree. There was an intimacy between them that had existed with none other besides Lady Barnes, but without the pleasure of sharing her bed. Not that he hadn't considered how good that, too, might be.

His valet, having decided that the day was better spent outside the carriage than within, had not been there to hinder their private conversation, which had been broad-ranging in topic and entirely nostalgic.

It had been lovely, one of the best trips in his memory. The year Maggie had spent with him at Ravenswood was one of the fondest in his memory, as well. Second only, perhaps, to the rare instances spent with his late mama in a good mood.

Maggie looked out the window, too, noticing his attention fixed on a point ahead and the slowing of the carriage. "Are we stopping here?"

He nodded, and noticed Maggie frowned.

She was more eager than him to reach the end of their time together. Yet Algernon wanted to linger in her company again tonight after dinner. Because, of course, their time of pretending to be husband and wife was at an end when he reached London tomorrow. After tonight, their last night together, they would go back to being near strangers, he supposed, and the affair would be over.

Algernon did not want to let Maggie go and never see her again.

He'd had no idea how much he had missed Maggie until he'd been given this opportunity to be with her again. When she was reunited with her father, he would have to behave as he left her behind. He sighed. Knowing there was no help for him to avoid that fate. He would not have her father believing her promiscuous because he was another man who would not marry her.

He was going to London to meet with the woman he might propose marriage to, as long as his suspicions proved false. But he already knew he wouldn't want to talk to Lady Kent all day like this, or perhaps even at all, if she became his wife.

Lady Kent was merely a means to an end. The only way to extinguish the large debts owed to his brothers.

That feeling of drowning, of being smothered by the weight of responsibility, returned to choke him, and he shrank against the back of the seat. Could he marry a woman he might never care deeply for?

Suddenly, Maggie's hand was on his thigh, and he turned to look into her worried eyes.

"What's wrong? Are you known here, too, and afraid you'll be seen with me? I could exit the carriage outside the village if you prefer?"

His panic only increased at that offer. "Don't even think about slipping away from me. I will come after you."

Maggie laughed. "I'm impressed you still think you can catch me."

Algernon had caught Maggie easily before, but then he hadn't seriously tried. Maggie hadn't been much of a runner, not that he held that against her when she excelled at so many other things. He had enjoyed their little competitions during their childhood. Maggie had arrived as a timid little girl at Ravenswood, and it was probably his fault she'd left nearly a hoyden.

At this inn, they would need to have separate rooms, due to the proximity to London, but he would pay her bill as usual. His way to thank her for returning to his life at this most difficult time, and showing him that the future could be better.

The coachman brought the carriage to a smooth halt before a fine-looking establishment he had stayed in before, and Algernon shuffled toward the door. "Maggie, would you mind waiting within the carriage while we secure rooms for the night?"

"I cannot afford this inn, either," she whispered, unconsciously caressing his thigh. The circling motion calmed him, but her touch also aroused him despite his best efforts not to be.

He shifted in his seat, knowing he could not act upon his desire. "But I can."

"How will I ever repay you for all this?"

He shook his head as Maggie finally stopped touching his leg. "Your company has always been repayment enough."

"Hardly, but we *will* talk about the debt I've run up later," she warned, glancing out the carriage door as well. "When I'm reunited with my father, though, I might not move for weeks. I feel like I am constantly on a ship being tossed about at sea."

He paused on the verge of getting out. "Have you ever been in a ship? I mean, actually onboard a vessel?"

"No, but I have read enough accounts of sailors returning to shore to know that it can take some time to find your land legs again. This is as close as I ever want to get to that."

Maggie had about as much experience with travel as he did, but she was better read on the subject, and a source of endless conversation about the world beyond England's shores. He deeply regretted that they would never travel to the places that fascinated them both, but he exited the carriage before he said anything that might embarrass her about her lack of funds and his endless responsibilities.

Sims rushed toward him, looking distinctly uncomfortable. "There is a slight complication," he whispered.

Algernon groaned under his breath. "Please don't tell me they have no rooms."

"Oh, they have room. One room only," Sims whispered again. "I took the liberty of claiming it."

"Then I don't see the problem," he said. "She will have the room."

"The proprietor of this establishment has exceptional eyesight, Your Grace. When he saw you and a woman alone in the carriage of the Duke of Ravenswood—her hand on your knee—he assumed she was your duchess."

Algernon gaped, utterly shocked by this development.

"I didn't know what else to say that wouldn't make it worse, so I went along with it," Sims whispered.

Algernon scowled at his valet with displeasure. "Why didn't you say she was my sister-in-law or a cousin?"

"Her hand was rubbing your leg," Sims said pointedly. Then he shrugged. "Besides, you are too fond of each other. I have sisters, cousins, and one sister-in-law who torment me. And I do not enjoy their touch at all. Should anyone else notice your fondness for each other, I feared they might assume she was not a proper *lady*."

Algernon heard the emphasis on lady, and nearly growled at the idea of anyone slandering Maggie Black's character.

"As a husband, you may speak with her, be yourself, and not worry about what other people think when you caress her hand."

"I do not caress her hand," he whispered heatedly through clenched teeth.

"I am sorry, but you *both* do without realizing you are," Sims admitted with a wince. "Not that I blame you, of course. She is lovely, and fond of teasing you. But I know you will behave respectfully toward her tonight when you retire together," Sims finished with absolute confidence. "The innkeeper will forget her face if you never stop here again."

The valet backed away, leaving Algernon squirming and with the uncomfortable task of confiding in Maggie about the continuation of their fake marriage.

He strode to the carriage, and one of the grooms snapped open the door for him.

"There is room," he told Maggie, extending his hand toward her to help her out.

She took it, clutching her travel case in her other hand as she stepped down.

Algernon quickly flipped her hood over her head to conceal her features. He took the case from her and thrust it at Sims to carry. "Follow us," he barked at the man.

Maggie was wise enough not to ask questions about the hood or his irritation with the valet in the inn yard.

Algernon led her toward the inn, nodding to the proprietor, but he did not stop to make conversation, and followed a deferential servant upstairs to their appointed room for the night.

He allowed Maggie to enter first, and she quickly looked around, her expression one of approval.

Sims directed Algernon's trunks to be set down in a corner, handed Maggie's travel case over, tipped the servants for their trouble, and then hurried everyone out of the room, quietly shutting the door behind them.

Maggie turned, clearly surprised to see him still standing there. "It's a lovely room, but why are you so upset with everyone?"

"I am tense because you're going to be angry with me." He went to one of his trunks and set his hat on top of it, trying to decide how to handle this situation. It was one thing to pretend Maggie was his wife under a false name, but quite another to have her addressed as his duchess.

Maggie finally noticed his trunks piled up. "Shouldn't your trunks be taken to your room?"

He winced. "They would if I had one. The inn had just one chamber I could rent tonight."

"I beg your pardon?"

"When the proprietor saw us together in the carriage, he concluded that we were husband and wife."

"Again, Algernon?"

"I could not correct his mistake because he knows exactly who I am. I'm prepared to let the mistake about our marriage stand, if you will keep out of sight for the night."

"But we are not husband and wife."

"Since I am known here by my title, I need you to convince others that you are indeed my..."

Her eyes bulged. "Your *actual* duchess?"

He cleared his throat. "The fib will ensure that you are treated better than you might have been in such a place, had our real relationship become known. Should I be asked about *my wife's* appearance on my next visit, I will say they misremembered."

She cocked her head to the side. "Misremembered? Algernon, are you married?"

"No. Not yet," he admitted, feeling ashamed

that he had not mentioned the purpose of his trip to London.

"Not yet?" Her eyes grew wider still. "What exactly is your status then?"

"Not married. Not betrothed," he confessed. "I am on my way to meet with a likely bride, though."

She reeled back a step. "You are on your way to propose marriage to another lady, and you want me to pretend to be her now?"

"We do get along quite well, so no one should question it," he promised, taking a step back from her. "It would just be for one last night. If you keep to this room, I will spend the night elsewhere."

"Where is elsewhere?" she asked, though her eyes narrowed with suspicion.

"Likely the taproom. That is where I will be going next, in fact. Until later, my dear," he said, backing up another step.

Her eyes narrowed dangerously. "You're leaving me already," she complained. "Hardly married two days, and I'm passed over for a tankard in a tavern and a serving maid on your knee."

She covered her face and broke into wretched sobs.

Algernon stared at her in shock—but then, she looked around her hands and winked at him.

There was no sign of tears in her eyes. It had all been a performance meant to torment him.

He laughed grudgingly with her and held out his hand. Maggie slipped hers into it, and he squeezed her fingers tightly.

"Why didn't you tell me?"

"I don't quite know," he whispered. "I should have, though."

Maggie winced. "Yes, you should have, and right from the start. I feel quite the fool."

"You're not the foolish one. You are funny and kind, and I know it was difficult for you to let me help you. I'm going to go and let you enjoy the quiet and respite from me, and travel. Sims should have gone in search of that bookshop we talked about by now, to make sure it is still there, but you don't have to go if you don't want to now."

Maggie bit her lip. "What if I want to see this fabled bookshop you promised to show me?"

"Then I will collect you in, say, an hour, and escort you there."

"I don't need your escort."

"But the wife of an important man does," he suggested. "The wife of the Duke of Ravenswood would never go anywhere unattended by her husband or a trusted servant. My mother had three companions who went with her everywhere."

"Ah, I see," she said, nodding. "And this is

another way for you to play the devoted husband, I suppose."

He inclined his head.

Maggie leaned close. "But what if you need protection from seducers. I am well aware that other women find you moderately appealing."

"Moderately? You wound me." He slapped his hand on his chest but laughed. "My dear girl, I have no intention of ever breaking my vows to you."

Algernon colored as he realized that what he'd said sounded like they were already engaged in a real marriage.

Maggie skipped right over his remarks. "You were always impulsive as a boy, Algernon, kind and thoughtful to a mere girl. You have always been so good to me." She stared at him a moment, and then a slow smile grew on her face. "But who, I ask, will protect *you* from *me*, should I suddenly decide to consummate our fake marriage?"

He stared at her in shock for a split second before he realized she was teasing him yet again. He laughed, disappointed that he could not consummate *anything*, and raised her hand to his lips to kiss the back of it. "Minx."

"It's your own fault, you know." She sighed heavily. "I only learned to misbehave because of you."

And that was sadly true. Maggie became his

match when it came to teasing. Always willing to give as good as she got. It was one of the reasons they had become friends so fast as children. The only person she hadn't warmed to was his father, and that proved her a girl of good sense. Maggie had always been wise beyond her years.

"I will give you an hour to lose your sea legs, and then I'll come for you so you can continue making fun of me while we find you something new to read on our continuing journey."

"I could go on alone," she suggested.

"No, you will not. Until you reach your father, you will be vulnerable to all kinds of indignities along the way. Besides mine." Algernon would make sure she remained safe as she traveled this last distance. She'd be under his protection, and he would not be taking advantage of that again.

And his reward...the pleasure of her company and witty conversation for the next few lonely miles ahead.

He kissed her hand again and strode out of the room, grinning all the way to the taproom.

He found his valet there in a corner, looking unusually glum. "Is she angry?"

"No."

Sims exhaled. "I was afraid I had spoiled things."

Algernon called over the proprietor. "A tankard of ale, sir."

"I wanted to convey my best wishes for your marriage, again, Your Grace, and hope your wife is comfortable during her stay with us. Should I send up a tea tray for *Her Grace*, Your Grace?"

Algernon glared at his valet and raised a brow, and saw him duck his head in embarrassment. He turned back to the proprietor. "Yes. My duchess does enjoy tea in the early afternoon." He supposed he would have to get used to saying that if he was to eventually marry Lady Kent. "Send up a maid with some little biscuits, shortbread if you have it. Oh, and a bowl of fruit: apple, pear, but not stone fruit."

"Of course." The proprietor rushed away to do his bidding.

Algernon glanced at Sims, who appeared to be hiding a smile. "What are you smiling about?"

"You do know her tastes very well."

"Yes, I suppose I do," he muttered, scratching his jaw, which required a shave soon. He was rather astonished that he remembered that tiny, unimportant detail from so long ago. "She hates oysters as well."

"Well, that's a shame for her husband," Sims quipped. "I hear that they can make a lady impassioned."

Algernon glared at his valet steadily.

"It's obvious you care deeply about her," Sims finished with a shrug.

"I do, and..." He pursed his lips and shook his head. "You seem to assume something could have happened between me and Maggie Black. But nothing has or ever should." He would not disrespect her by making advances she would certainly rebuff, now she knew the truth. He was lucky she didn't hate him for what they had done together already. "Were you not given a task upon our arrival?"

"I was, and it is complete," Sims promised, quickly finishing his ale.

Algernon raised a brow. "And?"

"The proprietor of Gill & Sons Bookshop is gratified by the Duke of Ravenswood's interest in his modest shop, and will wait for him and his beloved duchess all night if need be."

"She's not..." he said, and then swallowed down his correction. "I promised to escort Ma— *my wife*—there in the next hour, and we will *all* visit the bookshop together. It would do you good to turn your mind to something serious for a change instead of indulging in this ridiculous fantasy of yours."

Sims beamed. "Very good, Your Grace."

Algernon drained his tankard. Maggie was going to murder him eventually over this, or her father would, should he learn. However, he supposed pretending with Maggie was good practice for when he was actually married and had a duchess to consider the needs of.

A pity that when he said *my wife* and *my duchess* in the future, that the figure by his side would be his last choice.

CHAPTER NINE

"DOES Her Grace wish to venture an opinion on this book?"

"I trust your opinion, Your Grace," Maggie replied, keeping her face lowered. She'd never been a wife before, let alone a stand-in duchess, and she was highly embarrassed about that omission of Algernon's most of all.

It felt like an insult.

At first, it had been quite the lark, the idea of being an appendage to a husband who hid his identity as duke, and hers as well, on their journey. But now her mood had soured considerably, since he was openly referring to her as his wife and duchess while he intended to propose to someone else soon.

A wife was something she would never be. She'd always known that without money or great beauty, it would take exceptional circumstances to make a man offer for her. She had accepted she'd forever be a spinster.

But Algernon was known to many shop owners here, and the bookshop proprietor knew all about her before she'd set one foot through the door. Gossip in this town had spread like wildfire. The bookshop owner was practically rubbing his hands together at the thought of all the money he might make from the duke.

Maggie did not know how Algernon ignored the greed in the man's eyes, to be honest or the suspicious looks thrown her way due to her lack of finery. It had been hard to keep a civil tongue in her head as the man fawned over them both, though. Algernon was no man to be fleeced by any merchant who overpriced his books.

But when Algernon walked into a room, all eyes followed him. And because they did, Maggie on his arm as duchess was no longer invisible to others. She'd become someone worth noticing, too, much to her consternation.

The years she'd spent alone had not been easy. She had given up so many of her dreams. Yet no one had expected her to be anything other than what she wanted to be.

And now, because of Algernon, she was forced to play at being a duchess, albeit temporarily, and nothing in her life had prepared her for that development.

She glanced across at Algernon now, leaning against a bookcase, skimming a book that had caught his eye. He was a duke from the top of his head to the high shine of his polished black boots. No one could mistake him for a man of low importance.

He pushed away from the bookcase and showed her what he was reading. "You'll want this one, too."

She started to read and, after a few passages, took the heavy tome from him. But his hand settled under the book, covering hers.

Maggie found his proximity a trifle disconcerting, knowing what she did about his intentions toward another woman. But she read to the bottom of the first page, enthralled by the vivid descriptions.

Algernon's other hand curled about her waist and gently pulled her toward him. "Well? What do you think, wife?"

She wet her lips, struggling against the pull of need for more of his touch. "This is enough."

His fingers slid up and down her back. "What about the others I showed you?"

She looked at the short pile with longing, then shook her head firmly. "One and one only."

His hand dropped from her back. "I will buy them all," he announced. "A present for my beloved wife."

The wife he didn't have yet. The one he was on his way to court. Not really for her.

Maggie pressed her lips together, irritated with him anew and the ruse he played. She was no longer Maggie but some figment of his imagination. A wife was a creature she'd no chance of ever becoming.

Algernon's ongoing generosity was vexing and embarrassing. He should not waste his funds on her. She could not ask or expect her father to reimburse him for so much.

"Honestly, Your Grace," she complained. "I cannot accept any more of your gifts."

He ignored her words, settled the bill for all the books with the proprietor with a stack of coins, and handed the heavy books to the valet to carry.

He offered his arm.

"That was high-handed of you," she hissed, refusing his escort and tugging her hood closer to her head, despite the warm day.

"I've heard that before from you," he countered, smiling broadly despite her snub.

Algernon directed her outside and asked her to wait with Sims for a few moments while he went into another establishment alone. Sims had been shadowing them all afternoon, but he hadn't said a word to her directly since they'd arrived at this village. He looked uncomfortable, and she knew why.

Algernon had involved his servant in their lies. Maggie hadn't asked for help but was guilty of playing along with the duke's scheme to ensure her reunion with Papa happened quickly.

She caught Sims' eye. "Rest assured, I have no real designs on becoming a duchess."

The man's eyes widened. "I should be the one apologizing to *you* for the deception I forced him into. After all, it is my fault the proprietor believes you are a married couple."

Maggie stared at the valet for a long moment, and then shook her head. "His Grace said nothing of your part in this madness. It is just like him to take the blame, though."

The valet mumbled another apology, and Maggie nodded, accepting it.

"Well, nothing can be done to rectify the situation until I leave him tomorrow, I suppose."

Sims sidled closer. "I would not wish anyone to think the worst of you or my employer."

"Neither would I." She glanced around and sighed. The duke's game had to end, or he risked a scandal at the worst possible time.

"But I've never seen him like this," the valet confessed. "Not even with his brothers have I seen him so happy."

"His brothers *were* vexing as children," she noted. "I had hoped they'd be less so as adults."

"He's different with you. He's fascinated," the man warned. "He told the coachman to go easy on the horses each day to slow our journey, so he could spend more time with you."

Maggie straightened her spine, horrified by the confession. "I never asked him to do that."

"You didn't have to. He does as he pleases. The woman he intends to marry is nothing like you, either," the valet whispered.

"What is she like? Accomplished and elegant, I suppose."

"She's spoiled and ill-tempered toward servants. None of his brothers like her very much, but she's the money he needs in a wife."

Maggie frowned. "Surely money could not be his only reason to offer for her."

"I'm not sure His Grace even likes her," the valet whispered morosely.

Maggie was astonished by the valet's confession but attempted to keep the shock off her face. There were many reasons to marry without affection, but none she agreed with.

From the beginning, Algernon's words and behavior suggested he lived a carefree life. He'd been flirtatious, teasing, generous with her, and she'd responded in the same vein, imagining such foolishness that she could never repeat with anyone else.

Maggie's heart hurt, for him, and for herself mostly. She had become a distraction for Algernon again, but hadn't that been all she'd ever been to anyone? When he was married, he would forget her, but she would never forget him.

And she couldn't stand to watch him make a grave mistake.

She glanced at the bookshop window and realized what she must do. She asked Sims to wait outside before entering the bookshop again. The proprietor was only too pleased to see her return and answer her questions.

"Sir, have you a book of maps of the area between here and London I could consult?"

"I do indeed, Your Grace."

The shopkeeper was only too happy to oblige, and Maggie found the information she needed almost immediately. She stepped back outside and joined Sims on the pavement, pulling her hood back over her head.

Algernon reappeared a moment later, walking toward them with his hands behind his back and looking far too serious.

She squared her shoulders as he stopped before her and produced a posy of flowers from behind his back. "I recall you picked flowers from the garden at home as a girl. Did I remember the right ones?"

She took the flowers he offered and buried her nose in them, overcome by such a sweet, kind gesture...and the futility of it. "You have."

"I found some still in the pages of my books last month, when I reordered the library shelves. They made me smile, and perhaps it was an omen that we would meet again."

Maggie met his gaze, and her heart started to hammer against her ribs at the softer look in his eyes. He liked her, and perhaps too much. She gulped and looked away, lest she become lost in his gaze and make a greater fool of herself than she already had done.

Algernon's pretense was too much, too intense. Even as a faux husband, he was so easy to be around. He should be giving flowers to his future wife. Making his future duchess begin to love him, instead of Maggie.

"I have to return to the inn now," she declared, horrified by her last thought, pulling her cloak closer around her body as if it was all the protection she needed.

Algernon's brows rose high. "Is something wrong?"

"No, no. But I am eager to read these new books you purchased."

The books would be left behind when she

left tomorrow, hidden in his trunks, since she had the care of them.

Algernon shook his head. "But I had intended we walk through the town together," he argued. "The view of the river is quite breathtaking. Surely you could come and see it with me."

She should have said she had a headache, but she was a terrible liar, and he would certainly catch her out.

"The flowers should be put in water or they will wilt," she added. "You two go, and perhaps you'll find a better amusement than watching me read. I will be quite dull company for the rest of the day, I'm sure, with all these to look through."

"I have never once found you dull company, Maggie," he argued. "Even reading. If the flowers wilt, I'll always buy you more."

She looked up at him again, and she could easily see by the mulish set of his jaw that he planned to argue with her. He intended to take her along with him everywhere, as he had as a young boy. But she had to put a stop to their affair somehow. "I have no trouble with being alone, unlike some I could name, Your Grace. You do not own me," she whispered, and that made his nostrils flare. "Or have the right to say where I may go or not."

The duke's eyes narrowed dangerously, and he took a step in her direction.

Maggie stood her ground, determined to get her way in this. They battled wills silently, as they always had as children.

"Very well," he said finally. "Sims will escort you back to the inn and remain nearby to fetch you anything you might need."

"I cannot impose on his time. He should be with you. You are more important than anyone."

He looked about to argue, but Sims cleared his throat loudly.

Only that seemed to recall Algernon to their location. They were arguing on a public street, and if it continued, other people might notice and start gossiping about the Duke and Duchess of Ravenswood. He had wanted anonymity earlier, although by his actions in the bookshop, he seemed to have forgotten the reason for it.

"I will join you for dinner tonight, no matter what you say to the contrary."

Maggie inclined her head, resigned to that fact but not liking it. Algernon was currently paying her bills. One day, she would repay him for his generosity.

She wrestled the books from Sims, who reluctantly gave them up. "Take care of him," she whispered, before striding off toward the inn without looking back.

Maggie breathed a sigh of relief when she arrived back in their room without being followed. She put the flowers in water and packed the books away in Algernon's trunks.

Yet as she stood there, surrounded by his possessions and her one battered travel case, it struck her that their time together had been the happiest days of her adult life.

With him, she had forgotten her place, just like the last time they'd been together at Ravenswood. But her position in society was so low that they never should have known each other then; only Algernon could not seem to remember that.

But she did, and she was suddenly glad she might reach her father's current place of employment tomorrow morning. The map had proved it, only an hour or so away. But what if the duke found another excuse to delay leaving?

The loss of Algernon tomorrow might break her heart, but she had to let him go without showing how she felt. Because if she gave him any encouragement, and he responded in kind, she just might want to stay with him forever, despite the scandal of it.

And that was what her younger self had dreamed of doing—running away from her father to be with Algernon again. But she'd never found her courage in the end.

Maggie reached for the solace to be found in books, but had barely begun to read when the door crashed open and Algernon strode in. "I didn't expect our first fight to feel like that. Final."

She closed the book. "It *should* be final. I think you should go on without me."

"I'll not leave you behind," he protested

"But you will tomorrow. My father resides not far away, and he will expect his daughter to be dutiful and stay with him," she informed him. "Not consort with dukes about to be married."

Algernon stared at her. "You never mentioned we were so close to your father. Why?"

The why was easy. "Because I was not certain until I looked at a map. I had been enjoying myself for the first time in a long time. I did not want these days with you to end, but they will."

"They don't have to end," he said quickly. "I will speak to your father when we see him and encourage him to visit London."

"What else will you say to him? Will you tell him we played at being husband and wife and traveled alone together in your fine ducal carriage, without the benefit of a proper chaperone? Will you make him think that my headstrong ways encouraged you to ignore propriety entirely? We could stay a few days in another inn together, one with too few rooms, and you could buy me more flowers there, as well. Is it likely you intend to invite me to your wedding, too?"

He shuffled his feet and did not form a reply, other than a whispered *no*.

"Can you not see how wrong this has been?" Her stomach clenched at her foolishness, and his as well. "I'm certain your intended bride will be deeply offended if she discovers someone so unsuitable kept you from her side for so long."

"She will never hear about you from me," he promised swiftly.

Maggie winced. "So I am to be your last indulgence before marriage. I've always disapproved of husbands keeping secrets from their wives. What are you doing, sharing your confidences with me alone? You should buy *her* the gift of books! Do you really want to start your marriage with scandal nipping at your heels?"

He wet his lips and drew closer. "You are important to me, Maggie."

"I might have been once, but no more. You have slowed your journey, shortened your travel each day to accommodate a lady who is not a member of your family. You could have been in London already if not for me."

"You needed me."

She shook her head. "I could have made my own way, and you know it. Why do you delay?"

"I delay because perhaps I do not wish to marry at all!" he blurted out, then raked a hand through his hair. "She is but a means to an end. A way to set my brothers free of the great debt I owe them all."

Maggie gaped at him. "So it's true you're hunting a fortune for a bride? But Algernon, a marriage like that might deny you the chance to have the love you deserve," she whispered, horrified by his intention to make a cold-blooded alliance for money. "I would hope your brothers do not approve of this plan of yours."

Algernon glanced at her sharply. "It is my decision who I wed, no matter what they say."

"Well, I am glad they still want what is best for you, even if *you* don't. I cannot stop you from making a cold-blooded alliance, either, I suppose. But as much as I am concerned about your future happiness, our time together is at an end."

"It is over when I say so," he bit out, drawing close to tower over her.

Maggie lifted her face. He was angry with her now. He was a man who was never denied by any woman. But she *had* to deny him. She did not belong in his world. She never had.

"Algernon, would you truly want a lady to fall for you, knowing she had to give you up to another the next day?"

His eyes widened. "You love me?"

Maggie drew back from that question because she knew the answer would make this parting even harder. "I care for you a great deal, but any lady could easily imagine a future with you, and you know it. Don't make this harder than it has to be."

He stared at her, mulling over her words. "A gentleman could easily fall for you, as well."

"Well, it is fortunate I have no money to offer a duke in need of funds," she whispered, heartbroken over their parting. "I would have made a terrible wife and duchess, you know."

His eyes widened. "You would have been enough."

"If not for the money," she reminded him.

Algernon nodded and rushed out of the room. The door shut loudly behind him.

Their faux marriage now in tatters.

Maggie sank into a chair, suddenly bereft that she could never again speak with Algernon so freely. Tomorrow morning, she would set off for the next village on foot, if need be, without ever seeing him again.

It was the only way to survive a painful parting.

ALGERNON LAUNCHED himself out of the carriage the next morning as soon as it slowed enough not to break his neck in a fall. They had reached the village nearest to where he'd spent last night, and as he looked around, his temper did not improve.

Maggie had slipped away from the inn before dawn, or so he'd discovered after calling up to her room to tell her they could be on their way at her convenience.

Finding no sign of her had caused him an astonishing amount of unexpected panic.

But this could hardly be called a village worthy of being named such a thing.

A church stood at the crossroads and not much else besides. No grand houses for miles and miles. He scanned the nearly empty horizon, devoid of more than a few scattered cottages, searching for signs of life, but one most of all.

The innkeeper hadn't been able to keep the amusement off his face at learning a duke had lost his duchess, and had suggested groveling to win back her favor.

Algernon would not be groveling. He was more likely to put Maggie over his knee and spank her for frightening him to death once he found her.

He'd been unhappy that she'd taken dinner in her chambers last night after he'd revealed he was on his way to be married for money. Yet he had accepted her decision. He should have told her everything long ago. Because she'd believed him unencumbered by entanglement, they had become intimate, and that was entirely his fault. Acting as if they were truly husband and wife had clouded his judgment severely.

Yet he'd been sure a night spent apart would have restored her good humor with him, and they could continue on as friends. He still intended to deliver her safely to her father's place of employment, just to know what she found there.

And if, after meeting with her father, Maggie expressed a desire to visit London, he would have delivered her there himself, too.

And after that...he did not know precisely what might happen between them.

But she'd gone off without a word of goodbye, and he'd stormed out of the inn, barking out orders, berating his men for moving too slowly. His ill temper with her impatience continued unabated still. There was no reason for her to disappear like that just because he'd told her the truth about the plans he'd made for his future. Plans he'd made an eternity ago it felt like. And it wasn't as if he was spoken for already. He had uttered no proposal. He might still find another way forward without a great fortune at their disposal.

"Find her," he barked, and the grooms scrambled to do his bidding.

Sims paused at his side. "There's nothing here. Are you sure this is the place she was headed?"

"No, I am not. She conveniently never mentioned the name of her father's employer, either, only that she'd found it on a map yesterday and suggested that it was close. I don't even know where she came from. Obstinate wench."

He looked around again and hoped to see her appear just because he was there. He had to apologize, too. Clearly, he had enjoyed the experience, the novelty, of being in a fake marriage more than Maggie ever had.

Someone called out, "Your Grace!"

He searched for the source of the shout and

saw one of his grooms near the church, waving his arms and gesturing toward the chapel. He saw no sign of Maggie there but headed for the man straight away.

"Behind the church, just down the hill," the fellow clarified, when Algernon reached him. "I think it's your lady."

Algernon hurried in that direction and quickly caught sight of Maggie in the distance, sitting on the ground with her back to him. His breath caught, and he smiled in relief that he'd found her again.

Suddenly, Sims grabbed his arm, stopping his forward momentum. "It's a graveyard," his valet gasped.

His ill temper with Maggie vanished in an instant. But he shook off Sims and hurried on, anxious to see whose grave she sat near.

But he knew, deep down.

He knew she was looking at the final resting place of her papa.

Maggie sat amongst old, weathered head-stones, but the space immediately before her lacked any marker at all. The grass was absent over the spot and raised, as if the burial was very recent.

He stopped several paces behind her be-cause he wasn't sure if she had heard his ap-proach, and he didn't want to startle her. She did not turn, and in the end, he whispered her name,

"Maggie?"

"Algernon," she answered, but her tone was flat, devoid of her usual warmth when speaking to him.

He drew closer and crouched down at her side. "When?"

"Two months ago," she whispered.

Two months, and she was only just learning about it now.

Algernon gulped. "I am so sorry."

She nodded, and then shook her head.

Algernon glanced at the grave again. "How did you find him out here?"

"I asked for directions," she whispered. "The vicar told me where he was."

Algernon glanced back at the church and saw a tall, thin man standing about, talking with Sims. He turned back to Maggie. "I'll arrange a headstone."

"No."

Algernon put his hand lightly on her shoulder and squeezed. "He was important to me once, too. I want to do this for him, and you."

Maggie eventually nodded again, and he stood and left her sitting by the grave. He went to the vicar, and the man held out his hand to be shaken.

"Ah, Mr. Black."

"Algernon Sweet, Duke of Ravenswood."

The man seemed like any other country vicar he'd ever met. Plainly dressed and wearing a perpetually mournful expression. There was good reason for that today.

"I'm honored to meet you, Your Grace. A pity not to meet under better circumstances." The vicar smiled, though. "I was starting to doubt my letter reached anyone."

"What letter do you refer to?"

"Mr. Black spoke so fondly of his family and their achievements, and I wrote to the only address I could find in his trunk, yet received no reply. I could not believe his sons would not come to mourn their father. Did you receive my letter by mistake?"

Algernon was utterly shocked by the vicar's question. "Are you certain you buried Mr. Magnus Black here, and not some other poor fellow?"

The vicar appeared insulted. "I am certain of the name he gave me. It is written down amongst his possessions, as well."

"Mr. Black had but one daughter and no other issue. No sons at all," Algernon informed him, fighting his temper with the late Mr. Black.

"But that is impossible," the vicar said, sputtering. Then his gaze flickered to the small figure sitting by the graveside. "Oh, dear. I should have said more to comfort the woman."

Algernon ground his teeth. "Words mean very little at a time like this."

When his own father had died, Algernon could not remember a single word spoken to him. Nothing had made him feel different.

Their fathers were quite the pair. Cold and unfeeling. How cruel of Mr. Black to never speak of his daughter, his greatest achievement. He should have been so proud of Maggie, and told the vicar all about her brilliant mind and happy disposition. The vicar should have written to her directly, and not left her wondering all this time.

But clearly, Mr. Black had not written down *her* directions anywhere in his possessions.

"Tell me what you know about Mr. Black's demise."

"I'm afraid he died not long after he arrived to take up teaching at a nearby estate. He died in the night without warning. He had come here twice, on Sundays, so I knew him only a little. Never said very much about his own life, but spoke fondly of his hopes for his new pupil, and the other boys I had wrongly assumed were his sons." The vicar winced. "The family he worked for conveyed his body and belongings here to me and paid for the burial. His wages from his last employment were placed in his trunk by them, as well."

"Good," Algernon said, though he worried for Maggie's future even more now. A tutor earned very little, and Maggie was young and healthy. She had financial needs that must be met somehow. He winced, hoping Mr. Black had left her something in his last will and testament.

The vicar caught his eye. "You will find nothing missing, I assure you."

Not that they could know if there were items taken. They would have to take the vicar's word for it and hope he was as honest as he claimed. But just in case there was room for doubt, Algernon said, "I should hope not, or believe me, I will return to chastise the one responsible."

"I had his traveling trunks stored in the vicarage for the day his son, I mean his daughter, came to collect them," the vicar promised quickly.

"Sims will collect the trunks," Algernon demanded. "Now, I wish for you to arrange a headstone for Mr. Black's grave. He was sixty years old, born in Leeds, and for the inscription..." He thought a moment. "Magnus Black. Father. Teacher."

"Of course, Your Grace," the vicar agreed. "I'll fetch those trunks for you now."

Sims took the vicar away, gesturing for a few of the grooms to follow them into the churchyard to help carry the trunks. Algernon left them to it and returned to Maggie, who hadn't moved, other than to lower her head farther.

He stopped behind her, glaring down at the unmarked grave. "When my father died, I did not attend his burial. I have still not visited his grave even after a year."

"I don't know what to do," she whispered. "There is so much I wanted to say to him." She drew in a shuddering breath. "I was angry with him for so long."

"Fathers have that effect on us," Algernon agreed.

"He put every boy he met on a pedestal," she complained.

"Even I, and I certainly did not deserve it," he added.

"You were different. You wanted to be my friend and you were. That meant a lot to me. When the other boys were cruel, Papa always said it was *my* fault. That I provoked disagreement."

Algernon's temper returned, and he glared at the grave even harder. If Mr. Black had been alive, he would have given him the proper set down he so richly deserved for making Maggie feel inferior to anyone else in his life.

But Mr. Black wasn't here anymore. Algernon was, and he had to think of Maggie's needs today, and for the immediate future as well. Ranting at her dead father would not do her any good. She could not remain sitting alone in a graveyard. She might catch a chill.

He approached her and helped her stand, brushed off her long skirts, and held out his arm.

Maggie curled hers through his, leaning against him as if she had little strength left. After a few steps, Algernon slipped an arm around her back quickly, ready to support her on the way back to his carriage if need be. He was not leaving her behind. There was nothing for her here anymore.

He stopped and glanced back at the grave one last time. "Farewell, Mr. Black," he said. "Thank you for bringing Maggie into my life."

Maggie pressed her face into his chest but did not cry, and he led her slowly back to his carriage, avoiding the vicar entirely. By the time he got there, he was almost carrying her. The grooms stood in a line, hats removed, heads bowed in sympathy for her sudden loss. Sims must have told them what had transpired. What Maggie had found in this lonely place.

Inside the carriage, Maggie turned away from him. "You can leave me at the next good-sized town."

"I'm not leaving you anywhere, Maggie. We're bound for London together now, and I won't hear you say otherwise."

Her head rose a little. "Did anyone ever tell you you're impossible?"

"Not to my face yet, but that will never stop me from being this way. And in your case, we will inevitably argue about my behavior time and again. I help my friends, and right now, you need me."

Maggie had not always done what he wanted as a young girl. After a while at Ravenswood, she'd shown herself to be strong-minded and obstinate, not having anyone to tell her how young ladies were meant to behave, either. And that's what he'd liked about her most. She had never done what he'd demanded she do. She'd grounded him. Made him see that he could not always have his way.

But today he would.

When her head bowed again, Algernon could not stand to see her that way. She was not alone or without a friend.

He reached for her, gently pulling her across the bench and then onto his lap. She buried her face against his throat and held fast to him as he hoped she might.

He set his cheek to the top of her head and sighed. He would gladly give Maggie whatever comfort she required for the rest of their journey to London...and perhaps far beyond that moment, too.

MAGGIE BREATHED. In. Out. In. Out. But the discomfort around her chest remained the same. She stared at the ceiling of an elegant but unfamiliar room and listened to Algernon and his valet whispering by the door.

She didn't know what to do. Her father was dead, and she was all alone.

She ought to cry, but no tears would come. She hadn't shed a single one since she'd learned the news about her father. It was crushing to discover her suspicions were correct. Inside her was this vast chasm of nothingness now, where thoughts and anger over her father had once churned.

The door closed, and she slowly turned her head. Algernon was there, illuminated by firelight, silently watching her from a distance. They stared at each other across the room for a long time, and then he removed his coat, his boots, and climbed onto the bed beside her.

He lay on his side, not touching her or meeting her gaze, and eventually he reached for her hand to clasp.

She appreciated his silence and presence, because he was all she had for the moment.

He wriggled closer, pressed his head to hers, and kept it there.

Tears pricked the back of her eyes at the contact. Algernon was the best of men. Kind, considerate, and loyal when he had no reason to be bothered. A good friend, but a man she had to say goodbye to in the end.

He was going to marry another woman, no matter that it was wrong.

At last, the tears came. Maggie pressed her hands to her face, her composure undone by the warring forces of grief over her father and devastation over losing Algernon.

Algernon, unaware he was partly to blame for her tears, drew her into his arms and held her close against him, saying nothing as she railed silently about the injustices of her status in society. She was adrift, penniless and vulnerable. Her circumstances were unlikely to change for the better anytime soon.

But there was so much anger inside her that she almost couldn't contain it. She clenched her fists to keep her thoughts to herself, even as Algernon continued to hold her through the worst of the storm, rubbing her back as if she were a child again and lost in another strange, unfamiliar house.

She *was* lost.

She had no one but Algernon right now, and he was going to marry someone else soon, for the money they would bring him to pay off his debts. He could not help her for long. She had to find her own way in the world.

Eventually, her tears dried up, but she couldn't move away from Algernon's familiar presence yet. "Where are we?"

"Home. London. Grosvenor Square. Don't you remember arriving?"

"Not really." She felt herself dazed even now. "The last thing I remember clearly was you kneeling by my side at my father's grave."

"Understandable. His death was a shock. Before we arrived, though, you had finally succumbed to sleep. I carried you from the carriage and put you here."

"Thank you," she whispered, though shocked that hours must have passed since she'd learned the truth.

Eventually, Algernon loosened his grip but remained close. "I'll have tea sent up for you and then we'll talk."

"Yes, thank you," she whispered again, anticipating a discussion that involved finding her somewhere to live. She was tempting scandal and putting his marriage in jeopardy by even being here. He had come to London for the sole purpose of taking a rich wife.

Yet, she knew nowhere to go.

"I imagine you're not terribly hungry, but you should try to eat something, too," Algernon announced, forever bossy.

"Have I eaten today?" she mused out loud, but she hardly cared for the answer her stomach gave.

"I assume not if you cannot remember." Algernon was suddenly back and raised her face a little to press a kiss to her brow. "I'll have food sent up soon, too."

She could not eat. She wasn't hungry. With Papa gone, what was the point of even getting up again? Of hoping for a better future and regaining his approval. Papa had forgotten her, and Algernon would too, eventually. She had only herself to worry about now, and like Algernon, she needed money.

She was not above working for her supper, yet the skills she had in abundance were usually the province of gentlemen. Mathematics, science, and a fascination with history were not traits wanted by many employers.

Maggie exhaled a shaky breath and moved her fingers slowly over Algernon's chest. He stilled beneath her touch, and then covered her wandering hand. "You're spending the rest of the day here in bed. You don't have to do anything."

She bit her lip. She could not object when she had no better alternative. "Whatever you think best, Your Grace," she murmured, deferring to him because it was easier than making any real decisions for herself or her future.

"I trust I will not wake tomorrow morning to find you gone again," Algernon said.

"Where would I go?"

"You could go home," he suggested after a long moment.

She shook her head. "I have no home anymore."

He rose up onto his elbow, staring down at her with a sharp, indrawn breath. "I don't understand. You came from *somewhere*."

She glanced away, spotting her father's battered old trunks sitting on the floor by the window, with her solitary one on top. Embarrassment set in. "My father always settled some funds on me to pay for the little cottage he rented. Lately, he sent them in a letter. That's how I knew something was wrong. The money did not come last quarter. When I could not pay, the landlord evicted me. Everything I value, all I could carry, is in my traveling case," she whispered, humiliation making her face warm. "Though now I have my father's trunks to cart about as well, I suppose."

She would have to sort through her father's things, lighten the load, before she left Algernon, but she did not want to do that alone. Perhaps he could help her sort through Papa's things when he had time to spare. If he ever did, now he was in London to court his future wife.

"Oh, God, Maggie," Algernon whispered, pushing her hair back from her face. His fingers were gentle, and he refused to let her look away from him. "You should have told me."

He settled back beside her and brought her into his arms again, holding her tight against him once more. Maggie nearly cried for the warmth and comfort of his embrace, however temporary it would be. Somehow, Algernon could chase her worries away, at least for a little while.

"The last thing I want from you is pity."

He kissed her brow. "Good. Because I am not offering any."

She looked up at him, and then at his lips that had recently kissed her brow. They pursed as she studied them.

Maggie felt something twitch inside her, and she glanced down at his chest rather than examine her reaction or admit her feelings for him.

Algernon was handsome and charming. Her only friend in the world, and she, foolish girl that she was, felt drawn to him in hardly proper ways.

Algernon cupped the back of her head, unaware how that action made her pulse race. "You'll stay with me until we figure something out."

"I cannot do that. People will talk."

"You will stay with me, and we will discuss it when you're able to think more clearly," he insisted. He dropped another kiss on her brow. "For now, all I want you to do is stay right here in this bed with me."

She glanced at the trunks, and the thought of their contents caused her to tighten her grip on him. She did not want to consider what might lie inside her father's trunks. She did not want to smell her father's cologne. She inhaled Algernon's scent instead, a cologne that pleased her senses better. "Why would you want to help someone like me?"

"Because I like you."

She moved her hand on his chest, toyed with a button of his waistcoat. There was more to it than that. She remembered how he was before he'd learned her identity. He'd flirted and kissed her openly without knowing her name. And after, he *still* wanted to kiss her. "Do you find me attractive?"

"Without a shadow of a doubt."

"Would you kiss me again?"

"I would like to, yes," he said, but it sounded like she was being warned away. "But given the circumstances, I should not."

"I would like to be kissed," she whispered, before glancing up at him. "It would take my mind off everything I don't want to think about."

"Maggie..."

"Please."

Algernon sighed and moved toward her until their lips brushed. He drew back, as if a brief kiss was all he could manage.

She dropped her chin, embarrassed. "You did better when you didn't recognize me."

A short bark of a laugh left him. "I did not wish to presume too much by your request, not with the upset you've suffered today."

"Forget I asked," she said, and attempted to draw back from him.

"I can't let you go now," he whispered, and kissed her again, but this time with a great deal more enthusiasm than the first fleeting attempt.

She parted her lips and felt the tease of his tongue against hers. The thrill of it was almost too much. Her worries fled, replaced by the certainty she was where she was meant to be. In his arms. She had not been kissed often before Algernon came back into her life because, of course, her father had put a stop to any of her romantic adventures with young men and sent her to a place run by even older spinsters. When she was with Algernon, she felt young again and filled with hope.

Algernon cupped her face, wriggling closer as the kiss continued—deeper and more compelling with each breath. Maggie wrapped an arm about his waist and held on, causing their bodies to align perfectly atop her soft bed.

Algernon groaned, sliding his hand down her back, and he cupped her bottom firmly. He jerked her closer still until they were pressed tightly against each other.

Maggie moved restlessly, loving the feel of him so close, and also the evidence of Algernon's arousal. She wanted to be closer to him than anyone she'd ever known, and tilted her hips toward his.

Algernon jerked back instantly. "Forgive me."

Maggie blinked. "Why?"

"You asked for a kiss and I got carried away."

Maggie broke away from him and rolled onto her back, blushing and panting as if she'd been running a race. "I've always enjoyed you kissing me. Do you remember?"

"I do, but we were children then—mimicking

the behavior of adults with no understanding of what real passion was."

"We've always been good at pretend," she whispered, closing her eyes. Adventures with Algernon had always been a good distraction.

"I like kissing you." He admitted eventually. "But it should not happen again."

"A pity. I would enjoy more of your kisses."

"I will always want your kisses, too, but under the circumstances, I do not wish to lead you on," he said, and rolled off the bed. "I have responsibilities, and we are not children anymore. That kind of behavior, playing at being like our elders in the shadows of my mother's summer ball, would ruin you."

Maggie should probably be ashamed of herself for encouraging Algernon to misbehave. But it was clear to see, judging by their moment on the bed, that he was a skilled lover, and kissing had excited him, as well. She found herself smiling at what she'd done with him anyway. She'd rumpled him very well on this bed and taken her mind off her problems, at least for a little while.

Algernon looked even more appealing when his arousal tented his breeches like that, but when he noticed the direction of her gaze, he plucked up his coat and held it in front of his hips.

Unfortunately, desire had played little part in her life so far, and she did not know how to encourage him to feel better about what they had done. Clearly, he felt embarrassed when he desired a woman.

However, desire was a worthy field of study with the right man...if she ever found another one she liked as much as Algernon. Right now, that seemed unlikely, so she sat up and faced the window, giving him some privacy.

She sighed and stood, then kicked off her shoes.

"What do you think you're doing?"

"Well, if you don't want to kiss me, I'll need another distraction. I'll read a book," she decided.

"An excellent idea, I'll fetch the others for you. But you are wrong about what I want," he argued.

She moved around the bed, brushing Algernon's arm as she went.

He groaned.

She faced him, surprised by the raw sound, and saw hunger in his eyes. "Have I discovered a new way to torment you, Your Grace?"

"I would not do that again if I were you," he warned.

"What will you do? Kiss me or kill me?"

"Probably kiss you witless," he admitted, and then shook his head. "Forget I said that."

Maggie pressed her lips together over a laugh. The poor man looked shocked to have admitted to desiring her out loud. But Maggie was not shocked at all. She admired his honesty. "Don't worry, Algernon. I know a little about desire from books."

Algernon took a step forward. "Please don't tell me you've been reading about lovemaking all these years."

She smiled sadly. "All right, I won't tell you."

She'd rather keep him wondering for a while yet about her experience of men, anyway. He'd probably feel even guiltier for what they'd done together.

His kisses had been lovely, but there was definitely more to lovemaking than that. Her extensive reading had led her to believe it was an enjoyable way to pass the time. Maggie had lots of it now to spare. Why not give her innocence to a man she liked before they had to part ways? It was not as if he'd be betraying anyone yet. He was not betrothed at this moment.

Most likely, the chance to be with him would never pass her way again, either.

She put aside her disappointment and let the matter drop.

She collected a book to read and, on her way back to a chair, paused beside Algernon again. She looked up into his eyes, and she saw desire carefully banked there still. She was rather impressed that she affected him so much.

Since he wasn't about to help continue her study of desire tonight, she moved away and sat back on the bed, tucking her feet under the comforter. She understood his reason for hesitation. After all, he was probably used to women of experience, and some far more beautiful and accomplished than she could ever be.

Maggie would not offer herself to him again, no matter how perfect the moment might seem.

"I need to check on a few things downstairs," he said finally.

"Yes, I think that's a good idea." She did not look at him. She was starting to feel embarrassed, and it had created an awkwardness between them that had never existed before. "It was a difficult day. Please accept my thanks for your help."

"Always," Algernon promised, but shuffled his feet.

She glanced up briefly. "I promise not to leave the room."

"We will dine together, yes?"

"Yes, Algernon. I should like to dine with you," she promised. "I only hope the stew meets your high standards. I so hate to see you pout," she added.

Algernon took the bait yet again. "I do not pout."

Maggie laughed. "Got you again."

"Devil take it! You'll be the death of me, woman," Algernon complained, but with his easy laughter, the teasing mood between them had been restored. They were friends once more, and Maggie would not be asking for any further kisses from the duke. He was too important to risk losing over an idle fancy of hers.

He slipped from the room, and Maggie immediately put her book down to look around her properly.

The room was larger than any bedchamber she'd ever been in. The curtains were velvet and a dark shade of blue. The bed she was sitting in was huge. She had not noticed the size when Algernon had shared it with her.

As she gazed about, she realized that this might be the master bedchamber, if there were any personal items scattered about. But it was an empty room, bare and with an unloved feel.

Unsettled by that, she prowled the chamber, looking for...she didn't know what. Anything to tether her thoughts to the present. Opening each dresser drawer, she found them empty, until something fell inside one of the cabinets after she'd forcibly rattled a few drawers closed.

Opening it once more, she discovered an old property deed for a town house in London had appeared, as if from nowhere. When she looked closer at the paper, it seemed the top was rust-marked and torn where something once secured it. Strange that. She wondered why something so important had been left behind in this empty room.

Then she spied another doorway hidden behind a closed curtain. The door behind was unlocked, and it pushed open with a slight groan of the hinges.

Maggie inhaled Algernon's distinctive scent and immediately felt better.

Scattered about this room were comfortable chairs, with cushions galore and an odd blanket, too. A clock that had stopped sat on the mantle beside a box of cigars and a handful of scattered coins.

Beside the window wall, there was another doorway. Maggie found a large dressing closet, half full of male attire that could only belong to a duke.

Maggie glanced back at the room she'd been given and felt a sting of bitterness fill her anew. The room she had was clearly intended for a bride Algernon admitted not to love.

She hurried back to her own room—and was taken aback to discover Algernon there again.

"I thought that was you moving about."

"You heard me?"

He pointed to the floor. "My study is directly beneath our feet."

"I'm sorry if you were disturbed."

"In a good way, Maggie dear, and when have I ever denied you the opportunity to explore my home? I'm not about to start now."

"I was just…"

"Looking around my bedchamber. Peeking into my dressing closet," he teased, and then pointed around them. "My father did this, by the way. Removed any trace of Mama from this room as soon as she passed. Both here and in the country."

"That was cruel to you," she said, remembering Algernon's fondness for his mother.

"Oh yes, that was his intention. Sentiment has no place in the life of a duke, he'd always told me." But then Algernon smiled and nodded toward her hand. "What have you got there?"

She thrust out the deed. "Oh, I found this."

"What is it?" he asked, and held the pages up to the light. "Well, I'll be damned. Wherever did you find this?"

"Over there, I opened a drawer, heard it fall, and there it was." Maggie smiled quickly. "I gather it was nailed inside somewhere."

Algernon hurried over to the piece of furniture, pulled out all the drawers to look inside for himself, and then turned the bureau over, too, but there was nothing else to discover.

He sat back on his heels. "Sneaky, Mama. Very sneaky of you. I had forgotten my mother often hid things she didn't want Papa to have. This property was part of her dowry. Without the deed to it, he couldn't sell it to spend the profit."

Maggie nodded.

"Luckily, I have you to solve my mysteries." Algernon tucked the deed away in his pocket and held out his hand again. "Come, since you have regained your will to live and your boundless curiosity has solved a mystery for me, let's explore the town house together, so you won't get lost when I'm away."

Maggie was keen for something to do, and hurried to him. They toured the upper floor, but not the attics. "We'll save them for a rainy day," he promised, and then they descended to the first floor. "My study to the left, drawing room to the right. Other reception rooms farther back and below."

He let her take the lead, and laughed softly when she entered his library and gasped at all the books around her.

"I know where I'll find you, should you disappear," he teased.

"Or at any hour of any day," she warned.

"Such wealth. A book-lined room has been something I've always dreamed about having. A room where I would never be bored or lonely ever again."

He drew close. "Is it odd that I knew that?"

"Not when you know me best of all," she said without thinking, immediately regretting admitting so much. Her life had been quite lonely until she'd met Algernon again. And on her darkest day, when she'd thought he was better off alone, he'd come looking for her instead of going on with his plans.

She faced Algernon, but he was already looking at her.

His hand rose to cup her head, and he tilted her face up higher. "I am unworthy of the honor, Maggie."

She smiled quickly. "Don't say that."

"It's true. I kissed you, knowing all the reasons I shouldn't. I brought you here because I could not leave you behind, and I risk your reputation every moment we are alone. And yet I don't feel the slightest bit of doubt about my decisions."

She smiled softly. "Then you are exactly the same as the boy I remember so fondly from my childhood."

"I am not the same, Maggie. I know what

comes after kissing in a way you do not," he warned.

"Do you think to scare me?"

"I doubt you've ever been truly scared of anything I asked of you in your entire life, and that's what scares me the most." He sighed. "Maggie, I must go out for a while."

"You don't have to explain."

He nodded. "Will you be all right without me?"

Would she? "I will read."

"All right. Try to eat something while I'm gone, and don't wait up for me."

"Yes, Algernon," she promised, knowing full well she would remain awake until he returned to the town house.

CHAPTER TWELVE

THE WAY TO manage grief was to keep busy. Algernon had plenty of experience with that. When his mother died, he had focused on helping his brothers come to terms with their sudden loss. Inventing games, adventures, offering affection when needed, and, along with Nash, ensuring his younger brothers continued their education.

When father died, though, they were united in relief rather than sadness. Algernon only had to nudge them into action again, and they eventually found their true vocations and partners. It had been a satisfying endeavor, restoring order to his brothers' lives. But his work was done there. They had all married strong-minded women who suited their natures and kept them in line.

He watched Maggie picking at her food the next morning, her spirits low and her brow wrinkled by worry, and decided a distraction was called for.

He excused himself from the morning room table, pained to see that she barely noticed him going. He went immediately to speak to his butler to arrange for the carriage to be brought round.

"Shall I put the knocker on the door this morning, Your Grace?"

"No, I will be otherwise occupied today," he announced. He had confided in his butler about Maggie's recent loss, to explain her low spirits and presence in the house. He also explained that he'd known Maggie when they were children, and were still fond of teasing each other. Not that she seemed likely to do so today. However, he warned that she was used to speaking her mind to him and that she was not to be spoken of beyond the house on threat of dismissal.

Maggie just needed time and a place to grieve...but it was hard to watch, knowing of her late father's neglect.

Magnus Black, his former tutor, had been devoted to his profession. A true teacher in every sense of the word: encouraging to his pupils and committed to seeing them accomplish greatness. What he lacked was the ability to see that greatness existed already in his only daughter. Maggie could probably run rings around every pupil he'd ever had, especially Algernon, but likely never experienced a quarter of the praise from the man who'd meant the world to her.

It wasn't fair. It wasn't right. But there wasn't a damn thing that could be done about it now to set things right between them.

Everyone wanted their parents to be proud of them. Maggie had been denied that.

So had Algernon.

He returned to the morning room to find her still seated at the table. Her plate was no emptier than when he had left. He sat beside her and took up her hand and found it cold. He chafed it between his own hands. "I have errands to run."

"Of course," she said, blinking out of her daze. "I should go, too."

He squeezed her hand to keep her still. "That was what I was hoping you'd say. The carriage will be brought round in an hour for our outing."

"I meant, I can't stay here. I must leave. Find somewhere to stay in London and try to find a position. I have to earn my own way now."

He brought her hand to his lips and kissed the back. Unsurprised she had already formulated a plan, flawed as it was. "If that is what you want, of course, I won't stand in your way. However, I know you. You don't like rushing into any decision. Take your time deciding where to go. Stay here until you're sure."

She glanced his way. "What about your plans for marriage?"

He smiled quickly. "My plans are still plans at this time. I'm in no rush to reach the altar." Algernon could not think about getting married when Maggie needed him more.

"It is not like you to delay," she noted.

"Are you not pleased I am finally following your example to slow down and choose the right moment?" he asked, arching his brow.

A small smile touched her lips, and he counted that a great victory. "That would be a first."

He grinned widely. "Go fetch your bonnet and cloak. It looks to be a dull day out there, and we might be gone for a while. I want to show you all my favorite places in London."

She looked on the verge of refusing him, so he pulled her to her feet, spun her around to face the door, and set his hands on the top of her shoulders. Maggie allowed him to push her all the way to the bottom of the staircase.

The butler, at his post near the door, smothered a grin as he saw them together and wisely minded his own business.

Algernon removed his hands slowly from Maggie, although she hadn't protested his handling at all. "Go. Hurry, Maggie. I'll be here waiting for you."

She went upstairs slowly, though, and Algernon was unable to ignore watching her walk away. After their recent kisses, and last night particularly, the sway of her body had become rather more interesting than it should be.

He desired her, but he knew seducing her was unwise, and bad for *her*, particularly now. It was odd, feeling the way he did about someone he'd known forever. Her kisses had unsettled him more than they should have, and he was trying not to think about the chance of stealing another.

But this was Maggie, someone he cared deeply about and had for a long time. He felt as protective of her as he was toward his brothers. But it was not the same, and he knew that very well. He had to think of her reputation, her future, even at the expense of his own interest.

The butler approached, gloves, hat, and greatcoat in hand. Algernon took them, one by one, but his attention remained on the empty staircase as he waited impatiently for Maggie to return to him.

When he had proposed to bring Maggie on his journey to London, he'd never imagined the difficulty he'd face letting her go again. He liked having her near too much. Having her by his side to laugh with brought him a great sense of satisfaction.

Finally, Maggie returned, wearing the same

cloak over the same gown he'd first seen her in. Not for the first time, he wanted to do something about that. See her turned out in elegant finery befitting a lady of his acquaintance. Not that she would agree with him spending money on her, though. Maggie was brilliant but stubborn, and had fought against all his previous offers of help at first.

Providing her with a new wardrobe was bound to be refused, as well. And still, he knew he would do it. How to make her stand still for measurements by a modiste, and then keep the gowns, escaped him at the present time, though. He'd have to be sly about it, and have prepared arguments to convince her to accept.

He offered his arm but she refused him. They walked out of the house side by side, her with the hood of her cloak concealing her features, and he stood back as she climbed into the town carriage without aid.

Maggie took a seat facing the rear, and he joined her, unhappy with her decisions.

"What are your errands today?"

Maggie had always wanted to know what he was up to as a girl, and it seemed she still did as a woman in grief. "Gifts for my brothers' children first."

"Are you an indulgent uncle?"

He smiled. "I try not to spoil them too much.

Nash has two sons and a daughter now, so that is a great novelty for Ravenswood. The last young girl to reside there for any length of time was you."

"I was merely a visitor."

"For a year. A very happy year it was, too," he promised. "For me, particularly."

Maggie turned her face away, but soon it was clear she had become spellbound by the sights and muted sounds beyond the carriage windows. He watched her in silence, amused by the way her eyes darted here and there, drinking it all in.

Maggie had never said where she'd been living these past years without her father, but he assumed it was some small out-of-the-way place with few shops. A village that held no great attraction or visitors.

Eventually, the town carriage stopped before a toy shop. A place where he'd purchased presents for his youngest brother, Stratford, years ago. He climbed out of the carriage first, and Maggie refused his aid this time as well.

She scrambled out alone and looked at him expectantly. "What should I do?"

"Do?"

"It seems appropriate that I behave as a servant might around you while in London," she whispered.

"No one would believe you any servant of mine," he warned.

"They will if you try to remember I am beneath you," she suggested, folding her hands at her waist. "I am here to fetch and carry like any maid should, Your Grace."

She was there to be distracted from her grief and her plan to find unworthy employment. Her misplaced deference only served to annoy him. He would never allow Maggie to demean herself in such a manner.

He took a step toward her, determined to make her see the truth. "We are equals, Maggie. Submission does not suit you."

"No one but you ever believed I deserved more than I had," she said firmly, chin rising in defiance. "Not even my father."

"Arguing back only reinforces my opinion that you would make a poor servant. It is completely at odds with how a maid normally would behave."

"This is what must happen if I am to stay with you," she warned, jaw set in a stubborn line.

He drew breath to argue but decided against it at the last moment. She could play at being a servant for one day—but he would make sure she didn't want to continue by the end of it. A maid had a hard life. Up early, run off their feet, underappreciated, usually falling into bed exhausted late at night. Paid a pittance in most houses, and turned out immediately for any hint of indiscretion with a man.

A maid would never earn enough money or have time to spare to read, and certainly not continue their study of history, either.

He turned on his heel, snapped his fingers twice as he'd seen other pompous employers do, and expected her to follow.

Thankfully, she did.

Inside the toy shop, he took his time choosing gifts for his nephews and new niece, watching Maggie resist the lure of touching them all or voicing suggestions. Usually, she was no meek wallflower when it came to speaking her opinions, and he had to hide his triumphant grin as she shifted her weight from foot to foot impatiently.

He showed her nothing, did not speak to her directly or ask her opinion, which he found hard to maintain. By the end, the proprietor turned an unfriendly eye toward her, and Algernon pretended he did not care.

But then a small cast figure of a woman caught his eye, resigned to a spot behind the more popular toy soldiers. Only three inches tall, a woman with long flowing skirts and dark hair, reminding him of another piece he'd forgotten about until now. A toy Maggie had kept with her at all times as a girl. A piece his brother Jasper had thrown into the river at Ravenswood in a fit of temper with her.

It had unfortunately never been recovered.

His fingers itched to purchase the piece and right a wrong done to her so long ago. But today, he had to resist all sentiment, and turned away from it to complete his purchases.

The proprietor was overjoyed with his choices, wrapping each swiftly and making a great pile on the countertop. Algernon tossed some money at him, and when he left, he expected Maggie to collect the items.

She did not.

Algernon sent her back with a harsh rebuke for forgetting her duty. Maggie returned to the sidewalk, arms overflowing, face flaming as he told her to place the gifts inside the carriage and be quick about it.

When she returned, however, she offered him a hesitant smile. "Are you buying gifts for everyone in your family?"

"That would be absurd," he murmured. "There are over one hundred living Sweets in England."

"I meant your brothers and their wives, too. If Stratford may paint as often as he likes, he would surely enjoy a gift of brushes from you."

Algernon grunted at her timely suggestion

and marveled at her memory of their conversations. He did want his brother to paint a portrait of himself and his bride one day in the near future.

He turned away without further comment, walking toward another store and avoiding the one that sold brushes for painting, hating himself for what he was doing to her.

But he was determined to show Maggie that she wouldn't last one day as a servant. It was not in her nature to take orders or like having her suggestions ignored.

The next shop sold snuff, and although he did not use it himself, his sister-in-law did. He entered the shop and made Maggie wait while he considered the selections.

The strong smell of tobacco made his eyes sting, and he finally glanced back to see her discreetly wiping at her eyes. Was it the snuff or grief or both? He could not remember if her father took snuff, and hoped he'd not created a situation that had unwittingly caused her pain.

He completed his purchase quickly, glad to leave the stink of the shop, and heard Maggie exhale her relief, too. He sent her to the carriage to wait beside it while he visited a nearby coffee house, stalling for time. From inside, he could see her shifting from foot to foot, craning her neck to see what kept him from her side.

He laughed softly to himself, finished his coffee, and strolled back outside in no great hurry.

He gestured to Maggie to join him, making her walk along Bond Street as far as he dared, all but ignored. He was stopped by friends along the way. People he could not introduce her to. Talked of the city, politics, and world events. Many things that Maggie was sure to have an opinion about, but as a servant, she shouldn't comment on.

He hoped she'd had enough of the charade. *He* certainly had. If he saw her flinch again, he might forget himself and take hold of her hand right here on the street, just to see her smile once more.

He finally turned and headed back toward the carriage, only to spy a small establishment he'd forgotten about. Struck by an inspired idea, he headed to the shop, hoping his point had been made well enough that he would not have to continue this foolishness tomorrow.

CHAPTER THIRTEEN

MAGGIE SCURRIED after the duke from one shop to another, eyes wide at the abundance of both necessary and frivolous goods on display for purchase in London. She had struggled to keep up with him at times, as his longer legs ate up the distance easier than hers could.

Every time she found something to admire, he would abruptly decide he'd seen enough, and if the shop offered nothing of interest to her, he lingered there until she was on the verge of leaving without him.

If this was the life of a maid employed in London, she was certainly ill-suited to the position. Algernon had been right all along, and she realized his indifferent, haughty behavior that day was solely to point out the flaw in her plan.

She sighed when they stopped before another establishment and shifted her weight from one aching foot to another as she awaited his decision to enter or not.

There were no markings on the doors, and it seemed shabbier than the other places he'd patronized. But upon entry, she discovered a dressmaker toiled in this shop, and she looked at him in surprise.

However, the duke did not explain his reasons for being here. He immediately sought out the modiste and spoke only to her in so soft a voice, Maggie could not understand what was being said, not as he had done with every other proprietor he'd patronized that day.

The wealth of fabric around Maggie, all beautiful and exotic, claimed her full attention, and she could not resist touching some of the nearest examples on display. She became so engrossed that she didn't realize she was being spoken to until someone touched her sleeve.

A shop assistant stood at her elbow. Her smile was excited but hesitant. "Do you see something you like?"

"No," Maggie said quickly, folding her hands at her waist again. She did not want to offer the wrong impression that she could afford anything here. She was supposed to be a lowly servant in service to a demanding duke.

She cast an anxious glance at Algernon and

found him watching her with an unreadable expression on his face.

"What about this one?" the woman asked, presenting a bolt of fabric to Maggie for inspection.

The duke raised a brow, and she looked down.

It was a beautiful dark shade of blue silk, shot through with slub yarns that gave it a wonderful texture beneath her fingers. Maggie wanted it immediately for a new gown for herself. But of course, she could never afford it, nor allow the duke to think she might want him to buy it for her.

She shook her head quickly as she spotted a sly twist of the duke's lips before he turned away, fussing with something on the counter and pushing it toward the modiste.

Maggie glanced at the shop assistant. "It is very beautiful."

"The duke has approved any purchase of fabric you deem worthy of his sister-in-law as a gift."

Maggie blinked. "Sister-in-law?"

The assistant frowned at her. "Yes. The woman he's here to arrange a new winter wardrobe for. Please, something must suit. He has already paid the proprietor."

Maggie glanced over at the duke as he returned his hat to his head. "I will return in an hour," he said. "Make the choices. The modiste has the designs and how many gowns are to be made in each style."

Astonished, Maggie watched him leave the shop, oddly disappointed he was still purchasing presents for his family. But he was trusting her to make sensible choices for a sister-in-law, and that she could easily do.

She chose the dark blue silk and four other fabrics she was shown that would keep a lady warm for the coming winter. They were rather plain but practical, and easy for the modiste to work with.

Dress patterns had already been chosen by the duke, so she was not shown them. And since the duke had suggested she and his sister-in-law were of similar size and height, that meant Maggie's measurements would be taken, too.

It took a whole hour, and when she was done, she hurried outside, exhausted and wishing to return home. The duke was seated inside his carriage, and he was reading while he waited.

All the gifts he had bought today had been piled up on the rear-facing seat during her absence from the carriage. Maggie hastily climbed inside, resigned to sitting closer to him than was probably wise.

But thanks to her pretense of being a servant,

the camaraderie of their first days together was gone, and she desperately missed his warmth.

She turned her eyes from him and stared out at London's streets, which were alive with activity despite the leaden skies above. Her heart was weary again, and she sighed softly. They passed grand residences similar to the duke's, green squares, and dozens and dozens of carriages. The people, all going about their own business, hardly noticed the duke's carriage passing them by.

She sat back after a moment and found the duke watching her, his book closed but still in his hands. "It's something to experience, isn't it? London in all its glory."

She nodded.

"I wanted to be the one to show you around today," he admitted. "I know you're considering staying in London."

"I never said that I would stay," she said quickly, but where she belonged was certainly on her mind.

"You're sensible to be thinking about the future," he said. "If you're looking for a place to belong, London offers many opportunities for you, but not as a maid, I trust."

"No," she agreed with him. "I am ill-suited to taking orders from lofty men. I would also like something that will challenge me more."

The duke grunted. "What do you have in mind now?"

"Perhaps I could find a position with a professional bent."

He raised a brow.

"An assistant to a banker, or even a solicitor," she suggested. "I should have liked to study the law, but my father would not hear of it."

"You're smart enough for it."

"It is only an idea."

He nodded. "Did you enjoy meeting the modiste?"

"I spoke with the assistant more."

"It will amuse you then to know the assistant *was* the modiste. The older woman acts as the proprietor to ensure the modiste is treated fairly by her customers and isn't robbed blind. Society does not seem to value the creativity of young, ambitious women."

"Oh," Maggie said, saddened that the young woman had to pretend she was not the most important person in the shop. "The poor girl."

"Poor? That poor girl will charge me an arm and a leg to make those gowns as fast as I want them made. But her work is always flawless."

She looked at him in surprise. "You've purchased gowns there before?"

"For a past mistress," he confessed, after a slight hesitation.

Maggie blinked, and then shook her head. Of course, he'd kept a mistress in London. A duke was hardly likely to remain celibate.

"I send my friends there all the time," he confided.

"Your friends who have mistresses," she said slowly and then glanced over at him. "Do you have a mistress now?"

"No. I parted company with my last a year ago."

"Why?"

"It was time for a change," he said with a careless shrug, and then proceeded to describe their locations as the carriage made a slow circuit of the best neighborhoods nearest his. He even mentioned the possible wealth or occupations of the people who might live in each square.

None of them, the squares or the occupations, immediately appealed to Maggie. But not many women could have careers in this day and age. Gentlemen did, and she stored that information away in the unlikely event she ever needed it.

Eventually, the carriage returned to Bond Street and came to a stop before another establishment. "More shopping?"

"The best kind," he promised. The duke exited first and held out his hand to her. "Come,

Maggie, there is something particular I wish to show you now."

Maggie put her hand in his and he led her directly into Hatchards, a bookseller her father had spoken of with reverence many times but never brought her to see.

The bell on the door tinkled, announcing them. Algernon strode ahead to speak with the old man standing behind the counter—the proprietor, she assumed—and passed him something. He received a nod in return, and then leaned back against the counter.

The older man headed toward the front door and locked it. He pulled the blinds down as well and then came to her side. "Miss Black, please accept my sincerest condolences for the loss of your father. Mr. Black sent many a wealthy young man to my door over the years. Having you visit is the coup de grâce of my career."

She blinked. "Do you know me?"

"Your father spoke of you often. Regretted the shortcomings of his purse to send you all the books he found here for his students."

Maggie glanced at the duke and noticed he was shaking his head slowly. He peeled himself off the counter, sending the proprietor away with the flick of his hand. "We have the shop to ourselves to peruse for the afternoon. No one will see or distract you from your heart's desire. Consider it a belated birthday present, years of them, delivered all at once."

She rushed to him. "I don't need—"

Algernon put a finger over her lips. "Will you never tire of arguing with me?"

"Probably not," she admitted around the press of his finger.

His finger disappeared. "Then you will need to find a home with someone who will accept that habit of yours."

"So far as I know, that only describes you."

He pursed his lips. "You *could* work for me."

"I do not think that's..."

"Why *not* work for me? I pay well, and would allow you time for study."

"What position could you possibly offer me?"

"Right now, I need a secretary," he said slowly. "Sims has acted in the role for some time."

"Then you should promote him," she countered.

"I would, but then I would have to hire a new valet. I would rather do both after I marry."

"After I'm gone," she whispered.

"Two things I don't wish to discuss today," he said, and Maggie nodded, agreeing that the less said about the future, the better. It would only make the day sad.

She did not want to be sad.

She wanted to forget.

Maggie inhaled deeply and spun about, admiring the bookshelves. "I've no idea where to start."

His hands settled on the tops of her shoulders, and he pushed. "Anywhere."

She ran into a section, letting her fingers walk across the spines, reading as she went. She pulled out the first book that caught her eye and read the first few pages before putting it back. She continued that way around the large vaulted chamber, after noticing that Algernon was similarly engrossed across the room.

The bookseller came toward her, carrying a steaming cup of tea, and set it down on top of a stack of large books. "Have you found anything you want yet?"

"Everything," she said with a soft laugh. "But nothing I cannot live without yet."

Eventually, she did find a book that fascinated her, and she hugged it against her chest. Suddenly, Algernon was there, and he gently pulled it out of her hands before carrying it to the proprietor. She noticed him add hers to the other books that littered the countertop.

The duke had made a great number of selections. Curious about his choices, she went to see what Algernon had picked out for himself. She found they were all books that interested her, too, and she smiled.

"I should love to read these one day," she called out to him.

"You may read them first, since you are faster at it than I. Perhaps you will read some to me before bed."

Maggie noticed the proprietor glancing between them and smiling.

"It always gladdens my heart to see young people together who share a common interest in books," the man said with a wink.

"He's generous with everyone," she assured him, blushing as she returned to her perusal of the shelves around her. She and Algernon had many things in common, but none that did her any real good, and because of that, sadness crept up on her again, and remained with her for the rest of the day.

CHAPTER FOURTEEN

ALGERNON REGRETTED OFFERING to make Maggie his secretary at precisely six o'clock the next morning, because she woke him early and had bullied Sims into action, too, announcing that Algernon was to ride in Hyde Park.

He would also be making a call to his intended bride.

He rolled his eyes but complied, dragging himself from his warm bed. This was more the Maggie he knew.

He was dragging his feet on the matter of making a call to Lady Kent, since she was likely in Town already. He should have made it a priority to call on her sooner, but Maggie had needed him, and he had needed to be needed, too.

But now Maggie was making it *her* priority, and he would have to as well.

He rode for an hour in Hyde Park and returned to watch her bustle about the town house, moving purposely from morning room to study to library and back again, glad to see there were no tears in her eyes that morning.

Keeping busy had always helped him banish any black moods, and it seemed to work for her as well. Watching Maggie take charge of his town house, servants, carriage, and belongings was both fascinating and amusing for him.

He ate his breakfast alone but kept an eye on proceedings through the open doorways.

Maggie seemed to have a role that challenged her finally, though it was one that might never come her way in any other place. He was only slightly less worried about her future this morning. With her father gone, she *did* have to support herself somehow.

Maggie brooked no tardiness among the servants but listened to them with patience and respect. She seemed to be in her element ordering them about, and he knew he'd done the right thing for everyone's sake when the staff responded favorably.

When she finally returned to the dining room, hands on her hips, he pushed back from the table and stood. "Shall we discuss the day ahead?"

She put her hands behind her back. "Yes, Your Grace."

He held out his arm. "We'll adjourn to my study."

"His Grace should go first," Maggie murmured.

"Ladies first," he countered, leaving his hand extended, refusing to be ignored.

"I'm but your humble secretary," she insisted, stepping back from him. "I will follow behind you."

"Don't be ridiculous." Algernon barked out a laugh and grabbed her arm to thrust her ahead of him. He set his hands on her shoulders and pushed her all the way into his study.

However, he was not amused by her attempt at deference still. It did not sit well with him not to offer her any of the courtesies of a proper lady. When Maggie sat herself down on the chair before the desk, it seemed a misplacement yet again.

Sims arrived and sat close beside her, presenting all the correspondence he'd been carting about for Algernon since they'd left Ravenswood, acting in the role of secretary.

He began to describe the most urgent matters at hand, passing over the appointment book and other valuable papers Algernon had brought with him on this trip.

As the whispering continued between them for longer than he deemed necessary for the task, Algernon ground his teeth that he was excluded from the conversation. In fact, he suspected he could leave the room and neither would notice he was gone.

He had never imagined that making Maggie his secretary would deny him her conversation. Hadn't she, just two nights ago, clung to his body and asked to be kissed?

Of course, he shouldn't have kissed her then, and he silently vowed to do nothing else to bring about her ruin. She'd been disappointed in him, of course, but it was for her own good. And now he could hardly make love to his secretary. How would any work get done?

He sat behind the large desk, determined to suppress his irritation with the new situation he'd brought about, and opened a book to read while he waited for the pair to finish their discussion. They talked together exclusively for another half hour, and then fell silent.

When he looked up, Sims was gone, and Maggie was watching him. "Are you enjoying that book, Your Grace?"

"You should know I would, you read it last night."

"Yes, but I did not attempt to read it upside down."

Algernon snapped the book shut and threw it aside.

Maggie moved around the desk and sat on the edge. "You have changed your mind about hiring me already, haven't you, Your Grace?"

"Why do you say that?"

"You've been scowling at me all morning, and at Sims, too."

"Not *all* morning," he said.

"Particularly since we entered this study and started discussing your business and schedule for the next few days. You will be quite occupied, it seems, and given the tasks ahead for me, I don't think we will see much of each other."

Now he had another reason to scowl.

Maggie sighed. "You should have made Sims your secretary instead. He is quite smart and wants the position."

"But I offered it to *you*," he reminded her.

"And believe me, I am grateful for the opportunity to prove myself."

"I don't want gratitude from you," he muttered, and could not meet her eye. He looked again at the tired gown she wore with such quiet dignity. The small, pale hands gripping the edge of the desk. Hands that would not touch him again. "You've nothing to prove to me. What I want is for you to be happy and safe."

"I am safer and happier than I've ever been," she promised.

He looked up. "How is that possible?"

"Because I am with you, Your Grace," she said.

"Have you forgotten my name?"

"I forget nothing about you. But a secretary should not act so familiar with her employer," Maggie explained. "You cannot treat me any differently from any other servant."

He laughed at that and stood, crowding her against the desk. "I cannot see you any other way than I already do. We are friends, and we have kissed."

"But you don't want to kiss me anymore, which just goes to prove my suspicions were correct."

"What suspicions were those?"

Maggie, however, only shook her head stubbornly. "I can never be your equal. I am your employee now, and as such, I cannot expect deferential—"

She was too lovely, too appealing to let her continue with her misguided delusions. Too maddening and dear to his heart. He was drawn to her in a way he'd not expected to ever be with any woman.

It was a problem she seemed utterly unaware

of, though, as she continued with her nonsense about having no place in his life.

Algernon caught her face between his hands and kissed her soundly to silence her. Something he'd wanted to do from the moment their last kiss had ended.

He drew back almost immediately and looked down into her eyes. He saw the beginning of a blush forming on her cheeks.

"You were my friend first and always will be, Maggie. My equal. My superior in intellect. You will allow me to help you into carriages, buy you books, and you will sit beside *me* and not next to my servants in the future. I want to take care of you."

She stared at him, and then licked her lips. "Will you kiss me goodnight, too, and come to my bed at night if I stay?"

"No, that was our last kiss," he vowed, and then placed her in his seat behind the desk, aware that he was being bossy again but unable to stop himself. "While I might wish for more, I cannot ruin you. I cannot share your bed *if* I am to marry Lady Kent."

And there it was again.

If.

He'd said it out loud this time.

He'd much rather continue his scandalous

friendship, his affair with Maggie Black, than wed the wealthy viscountess he believed was the more sensible decision. It was a problem he had still to reconcile in his own mind, choosing between heart and head. He certainly could not have both.

However, the prospect of losing Maggie and their close friendship caused him the most concern. He needed her around much more than she seemed to want him. He could not have her take up a position elsewhere, so he would behave and cherish the time he had left alone with her.

Her expression remained serious as she reached for his hand. "I understand."

"Good." Algernon breathed a sigh of relief. He could not lose this woman. Not yet.

It was hardly proper for a duke to hire a female secretary, but he had no regrets about the bad example he was setting. It wouldn't be the first time he'd defied convention, or a member of his family had done so either. For now, hiring Maggie as his secretary was the only way to keep her busy, and in his life, and ensure she was treated with the utmost respect.

He glanced at Maggie now, studying her familiar face and expression. She seemed resigned to becoming a servant, and he hated that future for her. She deserved more, especially after all she'd been denied in her life.

She could have made a good match if her father had protected her better and provided funds for a dowry.

Clearly, Maggie had not noticed the same, or if she had, she was letting her past disappointment color her view of the future. He hung on her every word. Even Sims had remarked on Algernon's fascination with her.

He twined their fingers together. It was only when Maggie squeezed his hand back that he felt better about the future. "What plans have you made for me this week?"

She drew the appointment book toward her and studied the page. "You are long overdue to speak with Lord Thompson to discuss a matter currently before parliament. He's desperate for your support. I propose a dinner with him here tomorrow night would help you decide one way or another."

"Yes, he's been writing to me for weeks." He glanced at Maggie. "A dinner here at home is acceptable, but it will set tongues wagging and signify an alliance in the making. Though he will have my support in the end, I suppose. He also has a wife about your age."

"Jane," Maggie supplied.

"Yes, Jane. She might have come along with her husband, had I any family here to dine with us."

"Or if you were married," Maggie murmured.

He tensed and glanced at her. "Let us not discuss marriage today."

Not when he had significant fears about his bride's character.

"It is not a subject that can be avoided forever." Maggie glanced down at their joined hands. "I will have to add her name to your appointment book, and of course, the wedding date must be recorded in the family bible. Will you honeymoon with her as well?"

"Maggie," he growled, breaking away from her. He did not want to think of marriage, or his life after marriage. It would be so empty without Maggie's warmth and humor. The brush of her hand and lips against his.

He turned to look at Maggie. He knew *why* he was so filled with doubts about one woman, and not the other.

Maggie was the woman he wanted to wed. To share his life with. To take on slow journeys.

The longing for that was unbearable for a moment, and he swallowed back a curse.

He'd fallen in love with Maggie Black.

Twice, in fact. Once as the boy who'd been charmed by the fearless girl dumped at Ravenswood, and now by the woman who teased and liked kissing him. Nothing of that had anything to do with his title, his position in society, his family, or his quest for funds.

His heart wanted Maggie, but sometimes the heart didn't want what was good for the estate.

His estate, his family, his people depended on him to make a wise choice.

"Some women expect a fuss made of them when they wed," Maggie suggested, unaware of his inner turmoil. "A trip together could be a good start to getting to know each other better."

Yes, it had been in Maggie's case.

But Lady Kent still had a question hanging over her head. "I know Lady Kent well, and will soon know the rest about her. After I marry, we will return immediately to Ravenswood and settle into married life there."

Maggie nodded, and she tried to extract her hand from his. Algernon could not seem to let her go, though.

"Please, you're hurting me," she whispered.

Algernon released Maggie immediately and watched her rub her hand. He'd known that the discussion of marrying Lady Kent made him tense, but not *that* much.

"Forgive me," he begged. "It is a painful realization that my father still controls my life from the grave. In his last years, he deliberately ran the estate into the ground because I refused to marry his choice."

She winced. "Lady Kent was his choice?"

"No. His choice eventually married for love,

which I had discovered was on the cards sooner than he did, and I applauded the match. My father was furious when he found out and threatened to cut off my brother's allowance."

"All of them?"

"No. Just Stratford. Father knew where to hurt me most."

"I remember Stratford well," Maggie murmured. "He kept wanting me to carry him about or read him to sleep."

"I suppose that must have been a regular occurrence, thanks to your father's many employments."

"More often than I liked, to be honest," she answered. "My father's employers viewed me as an extra pair of hands they did not have to pay. I learned to be difficult to find whenever the family had very young children," she confessed. "The bothersome creatures never gave me a moment of peace."

He glanced at her in surprise. "You don't like children?"

"Not particularly," she admitted with a shrug. "To be honest, I should be happy to never have the care of one again."

His stomach pitted. His other reason for marriage was also to get himself an heir. Algernon was fond of all children, but he longed for his own most of all. "What about when you have your own?"

"I won't."

She could hardly avoid it if they married. "But if you did?"

"I cannot answer that," she said, shrugging again.

He drew in a deep breath and let it out slowly. "I've always imagined a small army of offspring running through Ravenswood's halls, bellowing at their cousins."

Her smile grew pained. "That sort of noise would be something to avoid, I should think."

A chasm opened up between them, small but significant. The first obvious difference of opinion since their reunion. Algernon had imagined Maggie longed for a family of her own, just as he often did. But if that was not the case, then...he was glad they had not been intimate yet.

He cleared his throat and hurried to change the subject. "What else is on my agenda for the coming days?"

She rattled off a list of things Algernon did not want to do, but he nodded to every single one.

"You should have those gowns for your sister-in-law by the end of the week," she murmured. "Should they be sent off to Ravenswood immediately?"

"No, keep them here," he informed her. The gowns and other items he'd ordered, a full wardrobe, were all for Maggie anyway. She would learn their true purpose only after they arrived, and he would not let her refuse a single thing.

He let his fingers caress her waist, feeling the coarseness of her current gown. "There are other fabrics I want to purchase later for my other sister-in-law. Materials better suited to an evening on the Town. We'll be in London for the season next year."

"I haven't the faintest idea of what is considered fashionable for ladies of the *ton*," Maggie argued. "I'm sure you do, though."

He grunted. She had a point. Maggie had not partaken of the season or spent any time among the cream of society in London during her life. Her current gown was serviceable but hardly first-rate. A fact he blamed squarely on her late and absent father.

Her current gown was nothing like what he'd want her to wear when she mingled in society as his wife. Something had to be done about her wardrobe *before* they wed.

Not *if* this time.

When they married.

Even if there would be no children.

He took a moment to consider his decision

and knew that he'd grown into the idea of making Maggie his duchess on their journey. He'd always believed in love matches. Didn't he deserve one of his own?

He rubbed a hand over his mouth, hiding the smile that came with finally admitting—he meant to make Maggie his duchess.

He would have to make a few adjustments to his priorities for the next few years, discuss everything with his brothers, and find some more money somewhere. He could certainly sell that town house Maggie had found the deed for fairly quickly, he suspected.

And with his marriage plans fixed now, he could devote the rest of his days in London to increasing Maggie's happiness. Her grief for her father would not go away just because they married. He'd probably have to wait out a period of mourning as well before he asked for her hand. In the meantime, he would continue to behave as usual. Turn her mind from plans of finding employment and keep her busy here with him.

"Please add a night at Vauxhall Pleasure Gardens to my schedule for this week. You will study what the fine ladies wear there, and what women of lesser status wear as well, so you are better informed when you return to the modiste."

She regarded him steadily. "You would be

better off visiting Lady Kent instead, while I endeavor to find out what other invitations she accepted for the coming week."

"I do want to see Lady Kent but at her home," he decided, reminded of the scandal he'd witnessed with his own eyes. "But I will require my secretary to expand her knowledge of society and the *ton* in keeping with her new role while I'm doing that. We will visit Vauxhall together soon."

"You're being high-handed again," she complained, crossing her arms over her chest and scowling at him now.

"Of course I am. That is what the nobility does," he warned. "I will have my way on this, Maggie, and reap the benefits in the end."

She shrank a little at his warning, and he did not like that.

"So will you, if you trust in me," he advised. "But, Maggie, I don't plan to stop being high-handed anytime soon, so you will have to accept that about me."

It would be a delicate line he'd have to walk, giving nothing away about his change of heart too soon. Maggie's life had been turned upside down with her father's death, and she believed herself unworthy of marriage. She could not see the happy future that he could yet.

Perhaps it was a mistake making Maggie his

secretary in the interim, but doing so kept her close. Love had found him, and Algernon would not let Maggie and happiness slip through his fingers.

CHAPTER FIFTEEN

MAGGIE PUSHED BACK from the duke's desk and stood, knowing there was nothing left to do that day until he returned. All correspondence had been opened, read, and set out in neat piles for his attention when he had a moment to spare. Algernon had been unusually busy and distant for days, preferring to mingle with society rather than be at home with her.

Not a word had been said about his courtship with Lady Kent, though, and she assumed he was meeting with the woman. Any day now, she expected to hear an announcement, but he'd said he didn't want to discuss his future marriage, so she did not dare question him again.

Though Maggie was incredibly curious about how the courtship was going.

Of course, her interest was entirely selfish.

No wife would permit Maggie to remain a secretary under her roof, or near her husband if she learned that Maggie had kissed him. But she enjoyed the work, expanding her understanding of Algernon's rarified world. He had so much going on, great debts, and she was gratified that he trusted her to know so much about his situation.

But it would all end when he married.

Not that she had any real regrets about her short-lived affair with Algernon, or that it had ended already. She couldn't help but like him still. She would have encouraged a courtship between them if he hadn't been born so far above her and desperately needed the funds.

She sighed and drifted out of the room, encountering the butler in the front hall, who only nodded to her and then went on his way again.

The servants did not seem to know quite what to make of her. She wasn't treated as a servant or even as a guest. She occupied a guest room now, but took all her meals alone since Algernon was always out at that hour.

Though she worked for the duke as his secretary, she still had the freedom to sit and read all afternoon, and all night if she wanted to, as well. The duke encouraged her to do as she pleased while he was away.

He claimed to appreciate her efforts to act as

his secretary, but if she faltered, it was clear that Sims would quickly resume the activities and be glad of the challenge.

Idleness did not suit Maggie at all, so she entered the duke's library and looked around for a distraction. The shelves burst with unread volumes, but she felt no immediate compulsion to pick up a book to read right now, and that was rare. She could not concentrate.

She had something on her mind, and today seemed a good day to close another chapter in her life.

She went upstairs, intending to return to her room, but stopped at the top landing when she heard the rush of footsteps. They came from the direction of the duke's bedchamber, though he was supposed to be out still. They came and went, yet neither the valet nor any other servant appeared.

Curiosity got the better of her, and she approached the door to Algernon's chambers, which had been left slightly ajar, to discover what was going on.

She put her ear to the wood.

One, two, three. One, two, three.

Was someone dancing in there?

She pushed the door open a little more, immediately spotting Sims twirling about on his own, with his chin lifted high in the air. His arms were extended stiffly, as if he held a dance partner.

He spotted her and came to an awkward, abrupt stop. He smoothed down his waistcoat and faced her. His smile was strained, his face flaming, as if he was fighting embarrassment. "Can I be of assistance, Miss Black?"

"Oh, no. I was just..." she stammered. "I just wanted you to know I have finished in the study for the day."

"Very good, Miss Black."

Sims was now a little more distant than he'd first been. Her appointment as secretary to the duke had caused a strain between them. She wanted to fix that, but it seemed impossible. "There was not very much mail of importance today," she told him.

"Sometimes there is," he answered, his tone clipped.

She bit her lip, worried that her elevation to secretary had truly offended him. "Perhaps you would care to glance through the duke's new letters yourself, just to be sure I missed nothing of great importance. I suppose he will not be back for some time to check himself."

He thought about it for a long moment, and then smiled a little. "It can help to know ahead of time what needs to be laid out for him for special occasions."

"I'm certain you have the right to look at his mail still." She smiled quickly, hoping that her suggestion would somewhat clear the air between them. She had not meant to exclude him. "Do you always practice alone?"

He swallowed. "Yes, of course."

"Might I make a suggestion?"

"Of course, Miss Black," he said, face falling.

"It is a small thing. When you do have a real partner in your arms, make sure to look down at her now and then. Women respond well to eye contact and the gentle squeeze of their fingers."

Sims laughed softly. "I had noticed that."

"I'm glad."

Maggie backed away from the door. Sims would never be a close friend of hers, but she liked the man. He was industrious, efficient, and usually quick to laugh. She understood why Algernon valued him so much, and she felt bad for taking away a position he'd aspired to.

She headed directly for her room and eyed her father's trunks, still stacked where the servants had moved them a few days ago, and rolled up her sleeves.

Then she took a deep breath and unbuckled the straps that bound the first one securely before lifting the lid on the contents.

Her father's cologne, the distinctive scent of him and books, hit her like a punch in the stomach. She steadied herself and reached for the first garment. His heavy winter coat seemed far shabbier and lighter than she remembered it being. Papa had occasionally wrapped her in it on particularly cold days when she was very young. But that had been a long time ago. Back when she'd been fussed over, and he'd truly seen *her* potential and not that of other people's children, as more important.

The shabby coat only served to remind her how much time had passed since their terrible argument. If he'd changed toward her over the years, she'd never know now. She fingered her years-old gown, too, the last gift he'd ever happily provided her. Affection from him had ended abruptly through no fault of her own because of one of his precious boys.

Maggie buried her nose in the fabric, overcome with bitterness about the past and assailed by fear and loneliness for the future. Her eyes stung with tears she didn't want to shed over him. She had to forget her disappointment, but she might never forgive.

She put the coat on her bed eventually, but as she looked up from it, she noticed Sims standing out in the hall, watching her warily. "Yes, Sims?"

"I heard a sob, and I was concerned. Is everything all right, Miss Black?"

"I'm fine, thank you." She smiled and gestured around her. "I am finally looking into my father's trunks."

He advanced a step to see them. "Might I be of assistance? I handled the emptying of the old duke's chambers for the family when he passed. It can be a difficult time."

"Well, then perhaps you can help me after all. I am not certain what to do with my father's old clothing."

"His Grace sent everything down to the servants' hall, and what was not wanted there went to the poor of the village."

Maggie nodded. "Could you help me with that? Making the offer and sending the unwanted items away?"

"I would be happy to," he assured her, heading toward the trunk and lifting out a shirt. "It has been my experience that clothing is the hardest for the bereaved. The smell, the reminder of happier times, tugs on the heart."

"Yes, I know what you mean. But there are few happy times that I remember now involving my father." Her thoughts about her father were still tied up in anger and regret over his distrust.

Sims nodded in sympathy. "Then I will make

short work of this and take them away imme-diately."

Maggie exhaled a shaky breath and stood back as her father's clothing was sorted, pockets checked, and then removed from the room.

Left alone again, Maggie peeked into the bottom of each trunk. Her father carried a lot of papers and journals with him. His lessons for his *precious* students.

Maggie considered throwing them all into the fire to burn, the way her anger still did.

Yet, his lessons had been her work for a time, too. Father had practiced all his lessons with Maggie first. Testing her and correcting his notes to help instruct others.

She had been his most constant student, and perhaps his smartest. Only Algernon's test scores had come close to hers, although she had no way to know how his most recent students had fared.

She set out all the papers, journals, and such by the age of the students he'd taught. By the time she was done, she had covered her entire bed, and the valet had returned.

"What's all this?"

"My father's life. Lessons. Study materials. Everything he took to the classroom and each new employer."

"May I?" Sims took a peek at one pile when she nodded, leafing through a book of instructions for geometry. "I had nothing like this as a boy."

"What did you have?"

"Apples, oranges, and my long legs to mark out feet and yards."

The simple image made her smile. "So you had an active education?"

"You could certainly call it that. After a while, I certainly ran away from the classroom more often than not. I do regret that of late."

Maggie frowned. "Why?"

He shrugged, and his eyes lowered. "It doesn't matter."

"I think it does. Tell me why?"

"The duke... I hoped he might have promoted me to be his full-time secretary one day, but he has you now, so he likely never will."

Maggie winced. "I'm sorry."

"It wasn't your decision."

But it was in a way. Her presence and Algernon's need to support her had deprived Sims of a chance for advancement. "I think... I think I won't be here for much longer, Sims."

He frowned. "Why would you say that? The duke has been clear that he wants you here."

She shrugged. "His future wife might have an objection to him employing a female secretary."

"No one changes the duke's mind once he's made a decision," Sims warned her.

But Maggie could, and had many times in the past. Eventually, she would leave the duke's employ, whether he liked it or not.

Sims returned the papers he'd been leafing through back to her bed. "What will you do with it all?"

Maggie shook her head. "I haven't the faintest idea."

"You could teach," Sims suggested. "Not that I want you to leave, of course," he added quickly.

"I haven't the patience for my father's calling," Maggie admitted.

"Perhaps another teacher would be interested in the material," he proposed.

Maggie shook her head immediately, though, disliking the idea. "My father was very protective of his methods, and would not have shared any of it with a rival tutor and have them take credit for his hard work. I would not like that, either."

"Seems a shame to have it all go to waste, though." Sims glanced her way suddenly. "Would your father have let others see his work if his ownership was clear?"

"I suppose he might have. It was not something we ever discussed." She tilted her head to one side, studying his excited expression. "What did you have in mind?"

"Publish," he said firmly.

"Publish?"

Sims nodded. "I have two older married siblings. Both have children of classroom age. They could never afford a private tutor. But books with lessons suited to each age would be of infinite value to them, and many other families, I'm sure."

Maggie mulled over the idea. "I don't know the first thing about publishing. I read books, not write them."

"You're smart and you learn quickly, from what I can tell," Sims noted. "Your father has done a lot of the groundwork, grading lessons by age, you said. But there is more work to do before it is suitable for widespread sharing, surely, and perhaps that would help you reconcile your loss. I'm sure the duke would undoubtedly help you if he's asked."

"I can't ask him for more help," she warned. "I owe him so much already."

"I think you could ask anything of His Grace," Sims murmured. "It is worth considering, and there could be money to be made from the enterprise, I'm sure."

"Oh," Maggie said, eyes widening in surprise that she had not thought of the benefits she might reap. If she could earn a modest living from instructing the young with a few books, then she would not need to rely on Algernon's charity much longer, or anyone else later, either. She looked down at her bed and blanched at the task ahead of her. "Where would I even start? I'm going to need your help, since this was your idea."

"What's all this then?" Algernon asked suddenly, startling her enough to yelp out loud.

"I was just helping her sort through her father's trunks," Sims assured him, springing away from her.

"Sims is brilliant," she enthused, once she'd calmed herself enough to speak. "He has come up with a way for me to support myself."

The duke glared at Sims as if he disapproved, and the valet started edging toward the door. "Explain, sir."

Maggie stepped between the two men. "I will publish my father's classwork as books and earn a living from the profits."

The duke entered the room fully, looking around first, and then at the overflowing bed. He picked up a lesson book and glanced at a few pages within. "I remember these. Your father guarded them like they were gold...but some of this is in your handwriting, Maggie."

"Not gold, but a tradable commodity for sure," she argued, ignoring his mention of her classwork. "Unfortunately, I don't know any publishers or how to go about finding one. Do you know of any?"

"No. Not yet. I have not had occasion to need a printer or met one socially. But it will not be difficult to find someone and make any arrangements for distribution."

"Distribution?"

He aimed a dry smile her way. "Well, yes. What did you think you were going to do after the books were printed? Stand on the pavement outside my town house and sell them like a poor flower girl must?"

"Well, I hadn't thought that far ahead," Maggie answered, disliking the idea of hawking the books one at a time. But she might have to do that in the end if she were to make any money.

"Clearly, there is much to consider and discuss about your project," he said, dropping the book back in its place and scowling. "That's why you need *me* to save you from the mistake and indignity of going into trade directly."

"I can't impose upon your time, Your Grace," she promised. "Perhaps Sims could help me a little?"

Algernon held her gaze longer than necessary in answer to her comment. The look said she would come to *him* first, Sims second.

Sims was sent from the room with a flick of the duke's head.

"This will take all of your time," he said, prowling the small room. Glancing into her father's empty trunks.

"It won't affect the performance of my duties, Your Grace," she promised.

Algernon stopped behind her. "I think it should."

She looked over her shoulder at him. "Why?"

His hands settled on her shoulders and squeezed. "Because this is the challenge you need in your life. A secretary is subservient to me. I'm not comfortable with that."

"It was your suggestion," she reminded him.

"To keep your brilliant mind from sadness over your father's demise and from making a rash decision. There's not enough of a challenge in my affairs to keep you happy for long. You need your own project to pursue."

"What about your need for a secretary? You *do* need one."

"Sims," the duke bellowed.

The fellow appeared startled by his abrupt summons when he appeared. "Yes, Your Grace?"

"Tomorrow, you will assume the duties of my permanent secretary, while you advertise for a new valet to take your place by the end of the week."

Sims glanced at her sharply, and Maggie grinned back, nodding, encouraging him to agree, not that she thought he'd refuse.

"What of Miss Black?"

"Maggie will need our help getting this lot

downstairs to the morning room, which will now be for her exclusive use as she prepares her subject matter," Algernon announced. "You can claim full credit for the inspired idea. Well done, Sims."

The valet grinned but looked slightly embarrassed to be singled out for praise, and rushed back into the room to collect the papers from Maggie's bed. She helped him return them to one of the empty traveling trunks and stood back.

When the bed was clear again, Algernon hefted the trunk alone and carried it from the room, complaining about the unexpected weight.

Sims glanced at the other trunk of her father's. "Should that one be taken, too?"

"Oh, no. It's just some old letters in there. I will dispose of them another day."

Sims rushed off after the duke, and Maggie followed them both at a slower pace, but her pulse raced with excitement and relief at having a purpose at last. Having a project like this could be just the thing she needed to fill her days in the long, empty years ahead. Publishing Papa's lessons would be no fast endeavor, but hopefully not a fruitless effort, either.

Algernon was still in the morning room when she arrived, watching Sims finish laying out her father's papers again, precisely as they had been sorted on her bed upstairs.

When he was done, Algernon sent him off to fetch tea.

"I cannot thank you enough for promoting Sims. He so wanted the position."

"It was the right thing to do. I'm only sorry I was not here to help you unpack your father's trunks." His hand rose to cup her face, and his fingers swept over her cheek. "You've been crying again."

"The unpacking had to be done, and I was ready to face it finally," Maggie told him with a shrug.

The duke set his hand on her shoulder and squeezed. "I would have helped, had you asked me."

"I know." She nodded and looked around. "But at least I finally know how I can fill my days."

"And mine, too. I will help you with this, Maggie."

"You'll be much too busy soon, I suspect."

"You will need finance to get started with your publishing," he warned

Maggie's excitement plummeted, but not her commitment. She did need something to do with her life. "Well, it will just take me longer, that's all."

"No, it won't take you longer than it needs to be. Not if we make this project a partnership."

She looked at him with surprise. "Partnership?"

"Business partners. You know your father's work better than anyone, since it looks like you wrote some of it, and can concentrate on making it suitable for publication," he said, gesturing to the papers littered around the room. "But I have the skills and contacts you need, and the money you'll require to get published as soon as possible. No half measures for this. The right word to the right people and the orders will come flooding in."

She gulped. "But you don't have money to waste on me. That's why you are marrying *her*, isn't it?"

"There is a world of difference between settling large debts and having the funds for a small investment like this. I can easily afford this new project of yours. I want to invest in your future, Maggie, but I won't dictate it."

She gaped. "I don't know what to say."

He winked at her. "Yes, Algernon, is always the right answer."

A servant arrived bearing a tea tray, and Algernon told them to set it down anywhere. Maggie noticed there were two cups, which meant the duke wanted to stay. Maggie's excitement returned, just knowing she had his interest and complete attention again. She had missed him greatly these past few days, and had feared that every conversation with him lately seemed like it could be their last. But now...

"Yes, Algernon. I would be very grateful for your help and a partnership to see this project through."

He winked again and poured her a cup of tea, just as she liked it made.

CHAPTER SIXTEEN

ALGERNON HAD NOT EXPECTED a party could feel so pointless, but it certainly was now he'd made up his mind to marry Maggie. He paused at the edge of Lady Kent's drawing room, nodded politely to a viscount's wife as she prattled on to another guest about the success of her eldest daughter's recent piano recital, and set his smile in place.

Across the room, clusters of fashionable men and women murmured behind silk fans or champagne glasses, sipping and watching one another with the sharpness of those raised on gossip and scandal.

And at the center of it all stood Lady Kent, smiling and lapping up the attention sent her way.

Algernon usually moved through society with the same detached focus he'd employed with his irritable father. Determined not to reveal his thoughts or provoke a temper with a misplaced remark.

But he was weary of it all and wished only to go home, where there was warmth and honesty.

He hadn't seen Maggie much today or yesterday. She had thrown herself fully into the work of compiling her father's lessons into publishable volumes, and Algernon had been out chasing down reputable printers for their project, too.

Maggie's absence by his side again tonight filled the evening with an ever-present ache, but could not be helped for the moment. He wanted further clarification of the scandal Lady Kent had created.

"Your Grace!" came the unmistakably sickly sweet voice of Lady Kent herself.

Algernon immediately extended his hand to her. The woman beamed him a smile, and he squeezed her fingers rather than kiss the air above them.

Lady Kent was as carefully constructed as the chandelier above his head: elegant, expensive, and ultimately designed for the prettiest display. Her gown was a white satin with silver embroidery that shimmered like snow. Her cheeks were rouged in the fashionable style, and her eyes glowed with the reflection of the diamonds at her throat.

"I feared you were detained again tonight," she said.

He *had* almost changed his mind about attending this party, in fact. The lure of a cozy night by the fire, reading with Maggie, had almost held sway. Algernon had not called on Lady Kent at home until tonight. But he had encountered her at other places and parties, dinners and such, where they had some opportunity to speak privately together.

His conclusion: she was desperate for a proposal she'd never hear from him now.

Coming here, though, would be seen as final confirmation that his interest in the woman was fixed. Everyone around them would expect to hear of a proposal tonight or very soon afterward.

Several gentlemen glanced toward them with mild interest, no doubt already bored with the rumor mill. Lady Kent had started one herself about his reason for returning to London so late in the year.

Algernon had done very little to dissuade the speculation swirling about Town about himself. So far, no one had noticed he was keeping a woman in his town house.

"Duty," Algernon replied. His duty to Maggie *was* his first concern now. There was much to be done before they married. He'd spent a few hours in a room at his club today, drafting terms for their marriage contract. Tomorrow, he would continue running the Archbishop of Canterbury to ground to petition for a special license for their marriage. He was regrettably unwell and seeing no one at present.

"I'll never be offended by you being a little late, my dear duke," she said sweetly, placing her gloved hand on his forearm without an invitation to do so. "I am delighted to see you at any time. London is rather dull without you."

"I am sure you were amply entertained," he said.

"Perhaps," she admitted, twittering a laugh that set his teeth on edge. "But you're here now."

"Yes, I am," he warned.

She tilted her head and looked at him with the coy smile of a title hunter. "What shall *we* do?"

He forced a smile. "For now, we make merry, but later you and I will have a little chat."

"You are as wise as ever to hold your tongue in a full room. I do so admire your restraint when we're in public together."

She didn't admire his restraint. She admired his title and the power she assumed came with it. He had once considered her boldness a benefit for a duchess—her confidence and beauty an asset, too. She was all things a duchess ought to be: well-connected, politically savvy. But she was also…a void. Beneath the practiced flirtation and prettily arranged smiles, she did not see him. Only the elevation of status he represented.

And if he had offered for her, her affections might never have been his alone, because the young man he'd met at the inn on his way to London currently circled the room in a servant's uniform, carrying a tray of champagne and offering refreshment to his employer's guests.

Algernon hadn't been noticed yet, but here was the proof of scandal he feared. "Would you care for a glass of champagne, Lady Kent?"

"Indeed, I would," she murmured in almost a purr. She glanced up at him and battered her lashes. "Shall we celebrate?"

"Not yet," he said, as he signaled the servant over.

"Champagne for the duke," Lady Kent informed the young man.

The poor servant only recognized Algernon at the last second. The tray shook, but no glasses fell, thankfully, as he gaped at Algernon and then tried to hide his shock.

Then they both glanced at Lady Kent, but the woman acted as if nothing was wrong with her young lover meeting the man she wanted to marry.

Algernon took two glasses from the tray and sent the fellow away with the flick of his head, as if he'd noticed nothing unpleasant. "To the future."

"To a happy future for both of us," she corrected.

"Indeed." Algernon thought of life with Maggie as his wife and sighed in anticipation.

Lady Kent glanced around at her guests with a smug smile that broadcast her belief that her wishes were about to come true.

She was proudly staking her claim by clutching his arm so tightly.

And Algernon let her think she'd won his favor, but his attention remained with the servant across the room, and his stricken expression.

Algernon stood beside Lady Kent for another quarter hour before excusing himself to find something stronger to drink. It was not long before he encountered the young servant again, saw him flinch at seeing him a second time as he asked for a brandy.

After he'd safely filled the glass, Algernon murmured, "Sensible people usually take my advice."

"I want to do that, Your Grace," he promised.

Algernon sighed, because the poor fellow looked frankly terrified. "If that is true, present yourself at my residence tomorrow morning," he advised. Algernon could find him a position somewhere else easily enough, even without a reference from his current employer.

The young man nodded then hurried away to continue serving others. As Algernon sipped his brandy and stared into the gold-tinged swirl in the glass, he considered what marriage to Lady Kent would have meant for him.

Her fortune would undoubtedly erase his debts and leave money in the bank for later years. It would have ended his anxiety over the viability of the estate. But a wife who dabbles with a servant was untrustworthy. Especially when it came to providing a much-wanted family and heir.

And she was no Maggie.

Maggie was real, warm, and funny.

And what would he give up, truly, if he chose Maggie instead of a wealthy bride?

The luxury of financial ease. Perhaps the support of some of his peers, his friends, in parliamentary debates.

He swirled the brandy again and took a long swallow. He would lose power. Status. Security.

But he might gain...everything that truly mattered.

"You look as if you are deciding the fate of the empire, Ravenswood," drawled Lord Varley, a good friend, coming to stand beside him by the decanters.

"Only my corner of it," he promised.

Varley nodded toward Lady Kent. "She's putting on quite the show for you tonight."

"Is she?"

"My wife was told there would be a proposal before the week is out."

"Was she?" He glanced around the room. "I don't see your wife among the guests tonight."

"Dreadful headache. I told her to go to bed without me, but she's likely waiting up to hear all the gossip when I get home from this. There's a wager at White's I'd like to win, by the way. It's up to ten thousand pounds. It's about you and her and wedding bells."

Algernon couldn't keep the scowl from his face.

Varley grinned heartlessly. "My wife tells me our hostess can spend the better part of an hour saying how well-matched you two are without mentioning your name even once."

Algernon shook his head. "Can she now?"

Varley poured himself a drink and gave Algernon a sidelong smirk. "You're not one to be led about by the nose when the stink doesn't suit you. What brings you here tonight, really?"

"That is an excellent question." He smiled but did not mention the scandalous affair involving Lady Kent and a servant that was playing out in this very room. "Oh, by the way, you'll be pleased to know we are officially neighbors."

Varley's brows rose. "Don't tell me you found the deed to the town house next door to me?"

"It was found *for* me," he answered, thinking of his great luck in having Maggie in his home still. "Now I must decide what to do with it."

"Do with it? Would you sell it to me?"

"If the price was high enough, I would." A property not entailed was a transient possession for a peer.

Varley nodded quickly. "I could be very generous indeed if it solves my immediate problem. My wife insists that her mother live with us in London, now that she's getting on in years. Imagine two wives trying to run the same household."

"And you'd rather have her in her own house," Algernon guessed, understanding in an instant. "I guess that explains your wife's headache."

Selling to Varley could be to their advantage, and especially his. The man was ridiculously wealthy but unfairly unlucky in his disapproving mother-in-law. "Selling Mama's property had always been a possibility once I had the deed in hand. But there is a chance that one of my brothers might want the property. I'll have to speak with them first before I make any announcement that it is for sale. However, I'm prepared to lease it to you immediately."

"You are, as ever, the best friend a beleaguered husband could ever hope for. If there's not going to be a proposal, I'd like to hurry home to tell my wife the good news."

"There won't be here," he whispered.

Varley rushed off grinning, but Lady Kent smoothly took his place. "Would you care to sit down, Your Grace?"

"I prefer to stand," he answered, wishing he'd left with Varley.

"You've been distant tonight," she murmured. "Is something on your mind?"

"Yes."

"You're thinking too much, Your Grace," she said, giggling. "I demand you stop."

Her giggling laughter grated on his nerves. "I often do think."

"But it's my party." She laughed and patted his arm when he didn't laugh along with her. "What is it that distracts you so much tonight?"

He drained his brandy glass.

She stepped closer, lowering her voice. "You know, you can always confide in me. We worry about the same things, I'm sure."

"What do you worry about?"

"Well, I cannot imagine it is easy having your brothers and their wives staying at Ravenswood for so long."

He raised a brow at her remark. "It is their home."

"But it must be vexing that the younger ones have taken such scandalous brides, and now the first one has returned, secret babe on hip. You must have been shocked like I was."

"Surprised, but I happen to adore their wives."

"Of course you do," she said, smiling. "I look forward to meeting them all soon. Perhaps at Christmas," she asked, brow arching in question.

Algernon was planning a quiet Christmas with just his immediate family, and Maggie at the heart of the festivities.

Lady Kent sighed as her young footman turned lover walked past bearing another full tray. "I shall be sad to never host another party here for you."

"Will you be sad to dismiss that young footman, too?"

Her gaze flew to her lover as he stood watching them across the room, ignoring the other guests.

She gulped. "Not at all."

"Husbands want no doubt that their heirs will be theirs alone."

Lady Kent blinked rapidly, and then her face paled. "Of course, Your Grace."

"Well, now that that's out in the open, I trust

there's no more that needs to be said about the matter," he warned.

She failed to meet his gaze and edged away a little. "I don't like what you're implying."

"Neither do I, madam. Seeing you pawing a servant outside an inn was not what I expected from you."

Her gaze flew to his.

"We will never speak of it or marriage again."

She opened her mouth to protest, but Algernon didn't remain to hear another word. He stayed another half hour for the sake of appearances, enduring several conversations with men who tried to pry into his plans regarding Lady Kent. Some were blunt, some outright rude.

"When's the wedding to be?" one foolish, drunken fellow asked.

"Wait and see," Algernon answered, finishing his drink but setting the glass down harder than he'd intended before he headed for the door.

At half past ten, he said good evening to a transparently frightened Lady Kent and escaped.

His carriage swiftly delivered him back to Grosvenor Square, and it was long enough to provide clarity of thought.

Lady Kent was a façade. Polished, smiling, composed—but an empty choice within. He didn't feel sorry for her. He didn't even particularly care what happened to her now. She was what his father told him he should want in a wife. What his debts demanded he acquire.

And yet, every time he thought of marriage, he thought of Maggie.

He stepped into his town house and breathed a sigh of relief when he discovered light shining beneath the library doors despite the late hour.

He paused in the doorway, gratified to find it occupied by his favorite houseguest. Maggie had waited up for him.

She was curled up on the settee under a large woolen blanket, hiding the dreary round gown she'd worn every second day, since she appeared to have only the two. She had a book open on her knees, and her brows furrowed in pretend concentration.

She only ever frowned when she pretended.

Maggie glanced up when he cleared his throat and smiled hesitantly. "You're home early."

"I was done." He came toward her slowly, removing his coat and rolling up his sleeves. "You waited up for me."

"I wasn't tired."

He admired her openly, his heart melting a little more. Her eyes were bright, but her fingers were smudged faintly with ink. He wiggled his fingers. "You've been working on our project again tonight, I see."

"Yes," she said, glancing at her ink-stained fingers, then reaching for a square of paper. "A note came from Lord Varley while you were out." She held it out, folded and still sealed.

He took it, broke the seal, and read it out loud to Maggie.

Your Grace,

I need to discuss an immediate lease of the town house next door for my mama-in-law, whether you sell or not. I'll call on you tomorrow morning to discuss terms.

Sincerely, Varley

Algernon folded the note with deliberate care and then laughed out loud. "Something disastrous must have happened when Varley got home tonight."

"Oh?"

"Lord Varley was at the party I just left. He slipped away early to tell his wife about the deed you found for me. His wife and mother-in-law must have started squabbling again. Poor man."

"I thought you planned to sell it."

"I probably will sell to Varley in the end, but first, I must discuss the matter with my brothers.

It occurred to me they might wish for the house to settle some of the debt."

"But you could keep it when you marry?"

He could if he wanted to. "Perhaps I could."

Maggie nodded slowly. She rose, smoothing her skirt down and looked up at him. "Selling is a good idea if you have no further use for it."

"I thought so, too. We, my brothers and I, each had our own little cottages in the countryside, but we all sold when the truth about my father's death was discovered."

"That was a sensible decision at the time."

Algernon dragged in a slow breath. Even with a short-term lease, before the sale of a town house, he still had insufficient funds to repay his brothers in full. But it was a good start. There would be other smaller opportunities to exploit in the months and years to come. He did not feel pressed down by the same panic he'd initially felt now he would marry Maggie.

"Maggie, I haven't proposed to Lady Kent."

"But you will."

"No, I don't think so. It was Lady Kent I saw with that young footman on our way to London. Her lover is in her employ. A servant I saw tonight, in her home."

"Oh," she whispered. "Oh dear."

"I require my heirs to be my own offspring, without any doubts in my mind."

"So you would have to begin your search for an heiress again?"

"No, I won't," he promised. "I want you."

Maggie stepped away from him, her body tense.

He followed her across the room, turned her about, and tilted her chin up. "What do you want from me, Maggie?" he murmured. "Because I think I'd give anything to provide it."

"What I want is for you to be happy." She reached up and laid her hand on his chest.

He brought her hand to his lips. He didn't argue. He just looked at her until her cheeks turned red. "I can survive the loss of a great many things, Maggie. But not a life without you."

Her bottom lip trembled. "Don't say such things."

He kissed her forehead. Gently. Reverently and then looked deep into her eyes. "Tell me this: would you be content living in the shadows of my life? As a secret?"

Her lips parted, but no sound came for a long moment. Her throat bobbed as she swallowed. "Are you asking if I want to be a kept woman?"

"No." His tone was firm. A mistress was the last thing he wanted. "I am asking what price I must pay for you. For your happiness, your pride, your company. Because I have decided that the cost of marrying for duty or wealth alone is too high for me."

The silence stretched between them.

Then she stepped closer. "I don't want to be a secret. I don't want to be a kept woman."

"I don't want you to be either one, but I want you."

He took her hands in his, the connection simple and searing all at once.

He nodded. "I've been afraid to reach for what I want. *You.* Only you. You were always enough, Maggie. You are much more than I ever deserved and all that I hope for."

Maggie's eyes widened and then she stepped back. "I'm going to bed."

He sighed, disappointed that she didn't want what he did...yet. Tomorrow, he would begin a proper courtship. Flowers and gifts. He already had the little figure from the toy shop in his room. He would convince her to imagine a much better future with him.

"Good night, Maggie."

"Will you join me, Algernon?"

He gaped at her in surprise.

When he ruined Maggie tonight, he would *have* to marry her. And when he married Maggie, he would gain so much...

He would be richer than he'd ever dreamed.

And that, finally, felt like his decision had been made.

CHAPTER SEVENTEEN

MAGGIE SHIVERED under the weight of Algernon's heated gaze, but she had made her decision.

Algernon. She had chosen him a long time ago.

She grasped his hand when he smiled and pulled him firmly toward the door. "Come with me."

"Maggie?"

"No questions," she whispered, turning back to him. She stretched up and pressed her lips to his in a hard kiss, so he had no doubts what she intended for them for the remaining hours of the night. "No debate, either."

"I can't promise you that," he answered, eyes lighting up with excitement that Maggie shared. "We tend to question everything."

"We do indeed." She tugged him along with

her. Algernon followed her up the staircase without another word. At the top, she had a moment of indecision, though. His room or her smaller one. But Algernon led her to the room adjoining his—the duchess' bedchamber.

It felt awkward to be in this room again, as it reminded her that Algernon had given up a fortune to avoid marrying Lady Kent.

But then he curled his arm about her from behind and kissed her neck, and her reservations fled.

Her decision to be with Algernon tonight had nothing to do with trying to compromise herself, or making a marriage with him, either. It had everything to do with wanting to belong. Here. With him. For as long as she ever could.

They had been circling each other and their desire since the moment they'd met again. Older, wiser, and more aware of each other physically. She wanted what she wanted.

Algernon. Kissing her.

The door shut behind them softly, and they were plunged into near darkness. What little moonlight came into the room from the window showed her where to go.

Algernon set his hands on her shoulders and steered her across the room toward the large bed. Then, before she could climb upon it, he pulled her back toward him and held her tightly. "We'll discuss terms tomorrow."

"Agreed," she said. But there were no terms to discuss. She gave her love without strings and wanted nothing more from him but his affection.

He drew back suddenly. "We could wait. We don't have to rush into bed together tonight."

"When have you ever wanted to wait?" she whispered, reaching for his waistcoat buttons and undoing a few. "Especially when we want the same thing."

"Yes, we do. We always have," he whispered, cupping her face in his hands. He kissed her softly. "I'll return in a moment."

He vanished into his chamber. He was gone only a short time. When he returned barefoot, he carried a candle that he set about igniting others with, until the room glowed.

Maggie had been comfortable in the near dark, but there would be no hiding from desire in the light.

Algernon returned to her, and he captured her head again, his fingers dislodging precious pins left and right as he buried them in her hair. "Maggie, be mine," he whispered.

"Yes," she whispered back. She stretched up for another, much deeper kiss to seal her vow. She would love him forever.

She slipped a hand between them, finished

unbuttoning his waistcoat, and pushed it aside to run her hands over his torso. He was muscled and lean and blazing hot to the touch, but still too far away. She'd found the baring of his forearms distracting, but now she wanted to see the rest of him.

His cravat proved impossible to understand how to untie, and he was the one who stripped it away and undid the tiny buttons on his shirt hidden beneath.

She grabbed a handful of his shirt at his waist and tugged upward impatiently.

Algernon grunted. "One button undone on my breeches will make things easier, my dear, or you'll wound me."

Maggie bit her lip and found the two large buttons on his breeches, as Algernon helpfully sucked in his nonexistent belly to give her room to unbutton him. Once they were undone, his shirt slid upward more easily.

When it was gone, she was confronted by a broad expanse of muscled chest and chest hair she'd not expected to see. She laughed at her foolishness. Of course, Algernon's body would have changed a great deal since he was a boy.

She placed her hand over his heart, and her stomach fluttered with renewed nervousness. She glanced up and saw Algernon smiling.

"Explore my body, Maggie," he whispered.

"Lovemaking is an adventure you've never experienced before. Nothing you do will be wrong, I assure you."

Comforted by his words, she moved back a little and set about doing as she pleased. She toyed with the hair on his chest, noticed it continued downward into his breeches, but his sides and back were silky smooth beneath her trembling hands.

She walked around him and couldn't keep the smile off her face. "You are beautiful."

"I prefer handsome," he replied, keeping track of her movements. "You are the beautiful one, my dear. Breathtaking. I was struck by instant desire the moment our eyes met across the crowded taproom."

When she stopped, Algernon pulled her in for another long, heady kiss.

Maggie began to unbutton her gown.

"May I do the honors?" he asked, and she nodded, giving him permission. "I've dreamed of this moment since the day we met again."

"So have I," she replied, glad they could talk and distract her from nervousness. It was one thing to *know* she wanted to be made love to, but quite overwhelming now that it was happening. Algernon had done this before; she had not.

He ran his hands down her back, and up again, and then seemed to be searching. Failing to find them, he suddenly spun her around. "How does this accursed gown unbutton?"

"From the front," she advised with a soft laugh. "I don't have a maid to help, so I had to improvise."

He turned her round again as she showed him the four simple fastenings that kept her breasts decently covered. There were other fastenings beneath, but all that was required was a hard tug at any bow.

He drew back. "Ingenious. I assume this is your design."

"Yes."

"Always clever, but you were made for more than needlework," he reminded her, before kissing her again.

Her gown was slowly stripped away, her shoes and stockings removed, and then Algernon drew back the bedding and helped her sit on top. He framed her face one last time, and then his hands were at his waist, unbuttoning the last fastening on his breeches.

He watched her as he inched the material down a little at a time. Maggie gaped as his erection was revealed, and she could not tear her eyes away even if a library was on fire.

He was unexpectedly large, though she supposed that was a good thing when it came to lovemaking. He kicked away his breeches, standing proudly for her to view. He even twirled around so she could see all of him at once.

Maggie was breathless when he finally stood still.

He climbed onto the bed, lay down, but immediately rolled onto his side, facing her. Maggie fell back onto the pillows and faced him, too.

He kissed her softly and then drew back. "There's still time to change your mind."

"Once my mind is set, there's no turning back for me. Or for you."

"I know," he said, and then kissed her again, with more passion than his first or last. Maggie wriggled until their bodies touched, and gasped at the feel of his hot skin sliding against hers.

Algernon radiated heat and excitement, and she couldn't get enough of touching him. She wrapped her arms about his neck and held on, letting him lead them in this intimate dance.

His hands caressed her in soft, sweeping touches, making her shiver. His lips devoured hers until she could think of nothing but him.

As he rolled her under him and widened her legs, she had but one moment of doubt, as brief as it was belated. She was a virgin, and some said intimacy hurt a great deal the first time.

Suddenly, he moved off her again. "Lovemaking shouldn't be rushed," he muttered.

"Was that warning for me or yourself?" she queried, taking a moment to catch her breath, too.

He laughed softly. "Me. All I can think of is making you mine. You are delightfully open to lovemaking, but as a virgin, there could be discomfort if I rush."

"I do know that," she told him.

"I'm glad you do."

He stroked down her torso, lingering to circle her breasts and then her nipples, until they grew almost too sensitive. "I can never get enough of touching you."

She glanced down at her bosom. Her nipples had hardened to stiff peaks and, to her surprise, Algernon kissed one, and then captured it in his mouth and suckled.

Maggie moaned, a guttural sound that shocked her to have made. She writhed beneath him, but he soon stopped and took her other breast into his mouth. She moved restlessly beneath again and held his head there, unable to believe how good it felt.

When Algernon stopped, he wriggled lower, pressing kisses to her stomach. Unfortunately, it tickled so much she giggled out loud and squirmed away from him.

Algernon captured her again and drew her back into his arms. "Your laughter is a sound I want to hear more of but later," he moved lower still and pushed her legs apart as he went. He kissed her thighs, lavishing them with his attention as he caressed them both.

She didn't comprehend his plan until the first touch between her legs caught her by surprise.

A kiss, a touch, and the flick of a tongue low down made her moan again. Maggie leaned up to see what he was doing.

She was shocked to see his face buried between her thighs. His eyes were closed, and he looked to be feasting on her. An action that felt strange, and wonderful, too.

She fell back, though, as he teased a finger along her sex and back again. Maggie was stunned as he excited her until the point she began to writhe, begging for more. Much more. "Algernon...?"

"Now is not the time for discussion. Just feel and let me show you what I learned about lovemaking while we were apart," he whispered.

The next moment, he kissed her sex harder.

Her hips rose to meet him of their own accord, and he wrestled her back down to the mattress, laughing softly. His fingers pressed against her body, and when the pressure increased too far, it almost immediately eased again.

Maggie thumped her head against the pillow, overwhelmed as Algernon turned her world upside down with his skillful lovemaking. She could barely keep still. She had never imagined making love would start like this, but how could it be wrong if it felt so good?

Each stroke of his finger inside her and flick of his tongue against her sex stole her wits. She could feel everything he did to her with a sensitivity she'd never experienced before.

She was about to burst out of her skin from what he was doing to her. When the sensations increased and grew too much to contain, Maggie squeezed her eyes shut and moaned as her body shuddered compulsively.

Suddenly, Algernon was above her, pushing her hair from her face, whispering, *"My Maggie. So beautiful. So perfect."*

She looked up at him, dazed, and smiled weakly, only to receive a hard kiss in return.

Algernon positioned himself to enter her, and she didn't feel pain at first, only a greater pressure than before. A hard thrust made her gasp, though, and he froze for a moment, withdrew, and pushed into her once again. He continued like that until he stopped to look down upon her, wearing a ridiculous grin.

He sank against her, brushing his fingertips across her lips. They remained connected, and Maggie liked that. "Are you all right, Maggie mine?"

She wriggled around him, testing the sensation of him inside her body. "I think so."

Algernon cupped her face. "Maggie, I love you."

She blinked.

"I do. I am in love with you. Probably since I was twelve."

Maggie did not quite know how to respond to that admission. Children hardly understood love.

But she did now. She felt loved by Algernon.

He began to move again, and it felt wonderful still. And as he made love to her, she realized this was all she needed to be content. To have a man, to have Algernon, be part of her. Intimately part of her life.

Maggie wrapped her arms about his neck, sensing his excitement rising, and held tight to him as they made love.

He moaned, buried his face against her throat, and after a few kisses there, began to move with even more urgency.

Those feelings he created with his fingers and kisses between her legs stirred again. Maggie rocked with him, wrapped her legs about his hips, seeking to experience a similar release again.

Algernon suddenly shoved her legs wider apart and withdrew from her completely. She saw the glistening length of his cock in his hand

and before his other covered the top. He moaned and pumped his length as he shuddered above her.

After a moment, he twisted to fall onto the bed at her side, panting hard and laughing softly. "My God, I love you."

"I love you, too," she whispered. "So much."

He kissed her hard but jumped out of bed the next moment, disappearing into his room again, his hands cupped at his groin.

Belatedly, it occurred to Maggie what Algernon had done. He had prevented his seed from filling her body and done all he could to avoid conception.

An odd ache settled around her heart at how loyal he was to their friendship, their love, and what she wanted for her life. Even in the heat of the moment, he'd put her needs first.

That was love, that was devotion...that was Algernon, her best friend and lover. Making love was enough for him tonight, but it might not always be so simple.

When he returned, he was wiping his hands on a cloth, which he tossed away before throwing himself back into her bed. He caught up her hand and kissed the back of it. "Now you really are mine, Maggie Black."

"Yes," she said, fighting a blush at how easy

he was to love. She would never take him for granted. Maggie rolled toward him, threw an arm across his chest, and held tight to his love.

CHAPTER EIGHTEEN

MAGGIE MUMBLED IN HER SLEEP, and Algernon couldn't tear his eyes away from her and the glimpse of her beautiful naked body. He had never seen her face in slumber. Her lips soft, her lashes thick on her cheeks, her dark hair wild across the pillow.

They were together, and his heart was full. Their lovemaking was all he could ask for. There had been a connection between them since childhood, and now it was amplified by their lovemaking as adults.

Maggie was the right choice, if he'd ever had a say in who he loved.

The only question left to decide was where and when to marry her. He considered a fast London wedding, or perhaps waiting to reach home and marry at Ravenswood, where they'd first met. But Algernon was not sure he could wait for the banns. He wanted to openly call her his wife, and for it to be true this time.

Algernon rested his head upon his bent arm, watching her until he could bear it no more. He slid a hand toward her under the sheet, poking her softly to see if she'd wake quickly or slow.

Maggie only twitched and then muttered something he didn't quite catch. She grew still again, so he pushed out his foot to touch hers.

She drew her legs up, her mutterings louder than ever. She said his name in a complaining tone.

He reached out and found her hand to hold. "It's morning."

"I can tell by the brightness." She pulled the covers over her head, though.

He leaned closer. "Do we want Sims to find us like this?"

The covers lowered slowly. "Probably not a good idea."

She sat up, then glanced down at her chest, her eyes widening. "I have never slept without clothes before."

"No?"

"No." She glanced his way. "I probably should be more shocked at us."

"I sleep naked all the time," he warned her.

An odd look crossed Maggie's face, and she blushed. He lowered the sheet a little more, and her eyes tracked his movement. Her lips parted as he showed her how excited she made him by just looking at him.

He laughed at her and drew her down for a long delicious kiss. Loving Maggie was so easy. However had he waited so long?

But he must take things slow with her this morning. She'd lost her innocence to him last night, and although she hadn't revealed any signs of pain, she might not yet be ready for a second tumble between the sheets so soon.

Besides, they had to talk, and he did that better with his clothes on.

Algernon tumbled about on the bed with her, though, distracted by the novelty of almost having a wife to hold.

He brought her beneath him and kissed the tip of her nose. "Good morning, my love."

"Good morning to you, too." She stared up at him, then cupped his face. A gentle smile touched her lips. "Algernon, what happens now?"

"We go back. Home."

Maggie sat up, frowning. "You want to take me home with you?"

"I was always taking you home to Ravenswood," he insisted.

"Won't your family object?"

"Not if they have any sense," Algernon

climbed out of bed and started picking up his scattered clothes. "They can either accept you as my wife or find somewhere else to live."

"Wife?"

He turned to look at her. "Maggie, why do you sound so surprised? Of course, I'm going to marry you."

Her eyes narrowed. "But you never said *the words*."

He tapped the bridge of his nose several times, berating himself. "So last night you invited me to share your bed, imagining you were to be my mistress or just a temporary lover I might discard? You said you did not want to be either."

"You said we were to discuss terms today," she protested.

"For the marriage contract that we will sign," he said, finding this situation highly amusing. "Are you going to deny me my heart's desire to make you my duchess?"

"I..." Maggie gulped and stared at him, clearly stunned enough not to form words.

"Good God, Maggie Black has been rendered speechless."

"I am." She stared at him and then a smile teased her lips. "Algernon, have you thought about this properly and what it means for you? For your debts."

"Hmm, not at all," he drawled, and shook his

head. "That's *all* I've thought about since we met. How to have you, not have funds to spare, and ensure the succession."

"Well, I know Lady Kent's behavior with her servant is beyond the pale, but there surely must be another heiress somewhere you could charm."

Algernon approached Maggie and got down on one knee.

"I, Algernon Sweet, fifth Duke of Ravenswood, do solemnly vow to love and cherish Miss Maggie Black for the rest of my life. Maggie, would you do me the great honor of becoming my wife and my duchess?"

"Algernon! You're naked," she said, glancing at him in astonishment.

"Naked or dressed, I cannot marry anyone but you. I will not. You said you needed the words and I will not allow another moment of doubt on your part. Maggie, I love you. More than life itself. More than even Ravenswood."

Her eyes filled with tears, and she reached for his hands. "And I love you, dear Algernon, but I would have been content with only your kisses."

Maggie tugged him up to his feet and hugged him tight. It was a glorious naked embrace that instantly aroused him. But there was plenty of time for lovemaking later.

"It was always marriage or nothing for me." He kissed her brow. "I'm afraid I won't be able to shower you with jewels and expensive new carriages, but I have lots of books and two full libraries. I promise to make you the happiest woman on earth."

"You already have," Maggie promised, burrowing deeper into his arms and wiping away more tears. "And I don't like jewels anyway."

"So, your answer, my love? I must hear it now or my heart will break."

"Yes, yes!" she cried, peppering his face with kisses. "A thousand times, yes."

He squeezed her tightly against him, heart soaring with excitement. They would be together and happy, and nothing would ever come between them.

They kissed deeply to seal their bargain, and then he gently pushed her back, only to see tears in her eyes. "What is this? Tears?"

"I thought I'd lose you to marriage," she admitted, sobbing anew.

He dragged a corner of the sheet toward them to dry her eyes. "No, my love. You gain me in marriage. Poor thing."

She gazed up at him and laughed. "You always know the right thing to say to amuse me."

Algernon beamed and kissed her cheeks. "Now, as much as I'd like to remain naked with you all day and make you laugh, it is time to put on your new clothes, and fix your hair so you'll be ready to meet one of my oldest friends this morning."

She looked up at him, clearly startled. "What new clothes? Algernon… Oh. Did you lie to me at the dressmaker about those fabrics?"

"I never said who the gowns were for, so I did not actually lie to you. But I don't know what the dressmaker might have told you about the purchase," he said, smiling cheekily.

She punched him lightly and then kissed his lips to forgive him. "That is the nicest thing anyone has ever done for me."

"That is just the start of what's to come, Maggie."

A great boom sounded through the house the next minute, and Algernon rushed to the window to peek outside. "Varley must really want to lease the town house for his mama-in-law to live in. He's earlier than he would usually call on me here. We'd best get dressed to meet him."

Maggie paled.

Algernon gave her a long, proper kiss to bring some color back to her cheeks and made her promise to join him downstairs soon. He would start small, introducing her to a few of his friends so she wasn't overwhelmed.

He hurried to his bedchamber, closing the door behind him to give Maggie privacy, and discovered Sims was already there, waiting with news of their visitor. He ignored Algernon's nakedness, but his gaze darted to the duchess' bedchamber door.

"Sims," Algernon called, and the man hurried into his dressing closet after him. But the look on his face clearly revealed his disapproval.

"Make sure Miss Black has the help of a maid this morning to dress in those new gowns I bought for her. When she's ready, escort her downstairs to the library with the maid as chaperone to meet with me and Varley."

"It's a little late for a chaperone, don't you think?" Sims muttered under his breath.

Algernon faced his valet after he'd thrown a shirt over his head. "Maggie will have no choice but to accept the help of a maid now. We are to marry."

Sims' face burst into a huge smile at the news. "About time!"

"Indeed, it is, but keep it to yourself for now," Algernon managed to control his grin.

"Congratulations, Your Grace. She'll make a remarkable duchess."

"Thank you."

Algernon finished dressing and hurried downstairs to meet Varley and found him using Maggie's eyeglasses to try to read the book she'd been holding last night, when Algernon had come home. "I had no idea your eyesight had grown so bad, Ravenswood. We used to be able to share eyeglasses, but these are impossible."

Algernon quickly took Maggie's eyeglasses away from him and put them in his pocket. "Your note sounded urgent, but not this bad."

"Oh, it is. My mama-in-law put a foolish notion in my eldest daughter's head that she could make her debut next season."

Algernon frowned. "Isn't she too young for that?"

"By two years at least!" Varley exclaimed. "And because my wife refused to consider the idea of an early season, the other girls are all in an uproar in support of their elder sibling. My wife has become the enemy at home and was in tears again this morning. I will not have that."

Algernon nodded. "A separation of mother and daughter is definitely in order."

Varley came closer. "So about the town house..."

"My only question is if it's far enough away?"

Varley huffed. "It will do for the immediate future."

Algernon named a monthly figure he hoped was not too high to be unacceptable.

Varley agreed without a qualm, and they shook hands.

A scuff of a shoe alerted Algernon that someone had arrived. He smiled and turned around, but he was not prepared fully for Maggie's arrival.

She wore a stunning new gown of deep blue, and her hair had been dressed, piled on top of her head with pearls. His heart started beating faster because of the smile on her lips.

Algernon fully approved of her appearance. He went to her and took up her hand. "Perfection."

He brought her into the room and presented her to Varley. "Maggie, this is Lord Varley. Varley, may I present Margaret Black, my betrothed."

Varley opened his mouth as he stared at them, but no sound came out. And then he started to laugh. "You devil! You could have told me last night you were engaged, but I see now why you looked so deuced smug. If I were in your position again, I wouldn't tell anyone I'd found such a beauty until after the wedding day was long over, too."

Varley came over and bowed to Maggie.

"It is a pleasure to meet you, Miss Black. My wife will be thrilled to learn I will win that wager at White's, as it is clear this will be the love match of the year, given the twinkle in my friend's eye."

Maggie curtsied to him. "My lord."

Algernon winked at Maggie. "There's a large

wager in the betting book at White's about when I take a bride."

Maggie nodded. "The *when* has yet to be discussed."

"Hopefully it will be soon for my friend's sake," Varley suggested. "But soon or late, I will still win. I might even be able to improve the pot with the right taunt or two."

"Don't push it too far," Algernon warned him.

"Well, this is good news all round." Varley snatched up his hat. "I shall happily install my mama-in-law next door and win the bet about you both, while I leave you to have the pleasure of charming this lovely lady."

Varley nodded to them and swept from the library, humming softly to himself.

Algernon faced Maggie. "You are stunning."

She blushed prettily and held out the skirts to twirl around. "Thank you for my new gowns. I had no idea they were for me when I chose the fabric I liked best."

"The bold color suits you. Thank you for agreeing to marry me," he whispered.

"About that..." she began.

"Large or small wedding?" he asked quickly, deciding not to leave any room for doubt that he would marry her one way or another.

She bit her lip. "What do you want?"

"I want you to be my wife," he said. "I do not care how we marry. Only *when* is important to me. I would prefer sooner rather than later, so the matter is settled. I will apply for a marriage license for us."

"That means we could be married as soon as you have the license, doesn't it?"

"Yes, we could, but is that what you want? I know you don't like to rush into things."

She wet her lips. "Under the circumstances, I think a private wedding would be less awkward for me. I have no one to give me away, or any family to attend a grand wedding."

"You'll soon have mine, but I agree, a small wedding is all we need." He brought her hand up to his lips and kissed her fingers, while he dug in his pocket for a ring to put there. He'd chosen one of Mama's rings for such an occasion. He hoped Maggie approved as he slid it onto her finger, relieved that it fit snugly in place. "There, officially engaged to be married. How do you feel?" he asked.

"Like I'm dreaming," she told him, giggling as she admired the ring. "Though I never imagined..."

"Well, you must do so now and often. There is nothing you cannot do or have from this moment on."

"Is that right?" She glanced at him with a

look in her eye that suggested she was thinking of what they had done last night, instead of things that might cost money.

He drew close to her. "If you look at me like that, my love, the answer will always be yes, by the way."

"That is good to know," she said, and grinned widely. "Do the library doors lock?"

He nodded and left her, grinning to shut and lock the library doors, before he rushed back to her side. "The marriage license can wait another hour to request, I think."

Algernon bent down and kissed Maggie, but this was no kiss intended to soothe. He cupped her head gently, determined not to muss her hair so early in the day, and held her close. Relieved that he would always be able to.

He was done fighting desire and yearning to belong to someone. Algernon's place was with Maggie.

He kissed her, unbuttoning her gown until it sagged around her bust and captured her breasts in his hands. Attempting to stem the passion Maggie had unleashed in him was no longer an issue.

He stroked the back of his fingers down her body and touched her left leg. Maggie did nothing to stop him. He lifted her gown until the bottom of it rested above her knees. Still, nothing he did seemed to cause her to have doubts.

"Maggie, you are too encouraging for my sanity," he warned.

"Well, a wife should be eager for her husband," she whispered.

She kissed him and used her tongue, teasing him and exciting him with no effort at all.

He got a hand between them and spread her thighs, impatient for what came next. Maggie moaned into his mouth and shuddered as he cupped her sex. He had to hear that sound repeated for the rest of his life, and set about making her moan again.

He found her entrance and probed gently. She moaned again and wriggled, giving him the access he desperately sought.

He pushed a finger inside her, even as he warned himself that he was going too fast. Yet Maggie seemed to accommodate him easily enough, pushing against his finger.

He drew back to watch her face. She had her lower lip between her teeth and panted at everything he did. The thought of her legs parted and her own hand there instead of his caused his cock to jump in anticipation of their future together.

He removed her new slippers, letting them fall away, and set one of her feet against his chest. Maggie nodded and lifted her other foot to sit against his shoulder, too, and slowly parted her knees wide.

The sight of Maggie like that, so open and aroused, gave him such a rush. He gazed down on perfection. Her body was waiting for him. The prize he might not deserve but craved.

He returned his finger to her sex, working it back and forth until he decided it was time to add another. Only when she was ready would he claim her again.

Maggie settled to lie back over the desk as he aroused her. When he thought she was ready, he had a moment of doubt. What if he got a child on her this time?

"Please," she whispered.

He could not refuse her. He unbuttoned his trousers and let his cock spring free. He'd never been so hard before, and it was all because he'd found the one. The woman he could not live without.

He fitted himself to her entrance and pushed with short, quick thrusts. Maggie opened to him easily enough at first, but then she hissed, and he backed off immediately.

"Maggie?"

"It's not you," she said, sounding testy as she reached over her head and presented him with a pearl-headed pin from her hair. "Dangerous things, hair pins."

"They can be," he said, as he pushed deep.

Maggie twisted her hips, settling him deeper with her movement. When he was fully seated, he lay over her and caught her eye. "Now what?"

Her shocked expression brought a smile to his face.

She swatted his shoulder. "Now is not the time to tease me."

"There's always time for that with us." He chuckled as he withdrew and thrust, but soon he was driving into her, unable to stop.

He braced his thighs against the heavy desk edge, changing position until she was aloft in his arms, and continued to fuck her even as he kissed her senseless.

Suddenly, Maggie stiffened, jerking around his cock as she climaxed. Algernon barely withdrew in time to avoid spilling inside her, too.

When he was done, spent, he set Maggie down to one side to avoid soiling her new gown. They leaned against each other, panting hard. Maggie started to laugh softly.

Algernon caught her eye. "What amuses you, my love?"

"I guess you're a lot stronger than you used to be?"

"That comes in handy when there isn't a soft bed around," he warned. "I've a book on the subject of positions for lovemaking that you might enjoy reading."

She clutched his head. "For the first time in my life, I believe I might be able to figure out intimacy without a heavy tome to guide me. Every passionate moment with you has been effortless."

He kissed her forehead softly. "Yes, Maggie, it feels that way for me, too, and always will."

CHAPTER NINETEEN

MAGGIE WOKE in Algernon's arms to the continuous sway of the ducal traveling carriage. She inhaled the scent of his body, noticed the warmth and weight of his arm across her middle, and sighed, blissfully content with her situation.

She was in love and loved.

She was a wife.

Even without the benefit of a marriage, she had given Algernon her heart and passion without strings. Their desire could never be denied. It was part of who they were to each other.

She glanced around at him to find him dozing, too, but then he roused and blinked sleep from his eyes.

"Good morning, Your Grace," she whispered.

"You have to stop calling me that. I will answer to Algernon, husband, darling, or dear. Not Your Grace or Ravenswood." She smirked at her husband's complaint even as he pulled aside the curtain to glance out the carriage window. "We're almost home."

Maggie's stomach flipped. She had become nervous about her reception at Ravenswood the closer they got to the estate. She hoped his brothers would not be difficult about their marriage.

Algernon insisted they wouldn't be a problem, and if they were, he was the duke. He could marry anyone he pleased.

But until she was certain how the news was received, she continued to worry. It was quite a leap from poor tutor's daughter to duchess. She had her work to focus on as well, and that also might be met with disapproval.

Her father's life's work was now her own. She was well into rewriting his lessons into pages suitable for printing. First, a mathematics primer for very young children. Then a child in the middle years. And lastly, another primer for the older children, those not yet old enough to attend university or who could not afford to go.

However, Maggie also wished to publish a more rigorous primer for exceptional students. She intended to have them all done in a few short years. And if she was successful, perhaps one day she could use the money to support the Ravenswood Estate.

Algernon would always require more funds to run the estate, and she was determined not to be a burden and contribute. He'd said the need for the money was not urgent, but the debt to his brothers would always weigh on him until it was repaid in full.

The carriage slowed and made a hard turn. Maggie hurried to open all the curtains to see outside.

"Ravenswood," she whispered, sighting green, lush fields and familiar woods.

"You remember now," he murmured.

"Yes, I used to dream about running through the woods with you."

His hand settled on her leg. "We could run about like that again, I'm sure, but perhaps since we're older, a walk will suffice."

"Probably more dignified for a duke," she teased.

"And a duchess," he agreed, laughing. "Oh, it is good to be home with you at last."

Maggie nodded, feeling excitement bubble up inside her despite her misgivings.

She had loved everything about Ravenswood as a girl. Well, except for her father and Algernon's. It had been her favorite place out of all the grand houses she'd been dragged to. And the closer they got to the sprawling country house, the more her memory of the place returned.

"It hasn't changed very much," she told him, sitting on the edge of her seat now.

"My father neglected the place in his later years, choosing to gamble away the money instead of making improvements here, and leaving me to pick up the pieces. There is much still to be done and always more on the horizon."

"At least Ravenswood has you to restore her to glory," she told him, covering his hand with hers.

Algernon drew her back against his chest. "A bit of advice before we arrive: no matter what my aunt or brothers say to you, don't take it to heart. You belong here with me. And if the old dragon, my aunt, doesn't approve of our marriage, *she* will be the one leaving. She still calls me *boy*, you know."

"Aunt Violet was the one who used canes on you, wasn't she?" she asked.

"Yes, she still swings them around. Hasn't hit anyone with them yet, since she needs the pair now to walk with."

"Good."

The carriage turned, and there was Ravenswood Palace, but it seemed smaller than Maggie remembered. Its facade was dulled by age and the late duke's neglect.

But then again, the last time she'd been here, she was a mere girl of ten and overwhelmed by the opulence around her father's latest employer.

In the years between her last visit and today, Maggie had gained more experience of the world of the aristocracy and wealthy landowners. She'd seen wonders and places she'd never dreamed existed, and suffered terrible losses, so she took nothing for granted anymore.

Especially not coming home to Ravenswood.

Algernon helped her from the carriage when it stopped before the front doors, grinning like the loon she adored with all her heart.

He held out his hand and drew her inside, speaking with the butler, whose face had wrinkled even more in the intervening years. Algernon asked for his brothers to be informed of his return, and his desire to speak with them immediately in his chambers.

Then he tugged Maggie directly toward the main staircase to take her upstairs with him.

Maggie rested her hand lightly on the mahogany stair rail as she ascended and allowed her fingers to glide upward, caressing the wood lightly like a lady should. However, the last time she'd been here, Maggie had slid down the banister on a dare. She'd been eager to keep up with her new friends, all the boys who had lived here, and it had been fun playing their games for a while—until it suddenly wasn't anymore.

She reached the upper floor, and they turned to walk along a hushed, carpet-lined hall.

Finally, he showed her into a large chamber.

"The master suite, I assume," she said, as she looked around.

"Indeed. Make yourself at home," he promised, before disappearing into what she further assumed to be his dressing closet.

Maggie wandered about, drinking in the contents of Algernon's private domain and the huge bed standing between two tall windows. The chamber was large and airy, full of light, with wonderful views down towards the distant lake. She went to look out the window and spotted groups of people clustered out on the grounds. They were too far away to identify, but they appeared to be picnicking.

She turned to ask Algernon about them when the door burst open, admitting a trio of men.

"About time you dragged yourself home," one yelled, and then disappeared into the dressing room.

None of them noticed her immediately.

"Well, where is she?"

"She is behind you," Algernon answered, and then reappeared with a man who could only be one of his brothers hanging off him.

The three men, three Sweet brothers she'd

once known as children, turned as one and finally spotted her.

She dipped a curtsy.

The youngest of them rushed over. "Maggie!"

She was swept up into his embrace and twirled around and around.

"I thought I would never see you again," he complained.

"Stratford, put her down," Algernon ordered.

"But it's Maggie, Algernon!" Stratford argued even as he obeyed.

"Yes, I am aware of that," he said, his lips twisted in a smug smile.

The one with the most serious face peered at her. "Why is Maggie Black in your bedchamber again, brother?"

Maggie lifted her chin. "You would be Nash."

He inclined his head but turned his gaze on the duke. Nash had never quite warmed to her, or understood Algernon's insistence that she join in their games as often as she had.

The third brother strolled closer, eyes narrowed on her.

"Hello, Jasper," she said politely.

"Mags," he drawled, smirking. "Good to see you back at the old pile. Here to stay this time, or just passing through?"

Maggie glanced at Algernon quickly.

"Maggie is here to stay," Algernon announced.

"Good, because the last time you left, two of my brothers bawled their eyes out for a whole month." Jasper came forward, caught up her hands, and surprised her by kissing her cheeks. But his touch, hidden from view of his brothers, traced over the ring on her finger as he whispered, "Stratford was almost as inconsolable as your new husband."

"She was practically our sister," Stratford protested, having missed Jasper's last remark.

"Never *my* sister," Algernon was quick to clarify with a wink for her, but then whatever he might have said next was cut off by the sound of breaking glass.

Algernon dashed to the window to look outside.

Nash, however, pinched the bridge of his nose. "Not another window. Why can they not be satisfied with bowls instead of cricket?"

"What the devil is going on here? Who are those people?"

Jasper groaned. "Our aunt is still hosting that little family gathering you agreed to let her have."

"Little? There are..." Algernon started, as he started to count, pointing his finger.

"Fifty-three adults and a dozen younger ones

in the nursery, all told, plus servants, horses, and dogs. Lots of unruly, barking dogs."

Algernon turned, face pale, eyes wild. "I did *not* agree to this. Is she trying to bankrupt me?"

Jasper shrugged. "Who knows what the old dragon wants. I try to stay out of her way as much as possible. She's still too fond of swinging those canes for my taste."

Maggie bit her lip to hold in her thoughts about Aunt Violet and her canes. It was not her place to venture an opinion on family matters so soon. But Aunt Violet needed to be put in her place eventually.

"I'll deal with her," Algernon growled.

"We'll keep Maggie company while you tackle the dragon," Jasper promised.

"No." Algernon shook his head. "She'll need to meet my duchess eventually."

Maggie did not remind him that she was already well acquainted with his aunt Violet and her canes. But before she met anyone else, she needed a moment or two in private to prepare. "If you could show me to my room, I'd like to freshen up first."

"Yes, of course, my love" Algernon murmured. "Your trunks should have been brought up already, and I had the butler send up water, too. Come this way, my dear, and I'll show you your bedchamber."

Behind them, she heard Stratford whisper, "Did he just say her bedchamber?"

"He did indeed," Jasper said, not bothering to lower his voice. "Didn't you notice the ring on her finger? Do try to catch up."

"Our brother has made a surprising choice indeed. I'll find out why later," Nash announced, as they moved as one to look into her new chamber.

Jasper snorted. "Isn't it obvious?"

Maggie turned and kissed Algernon full on the lips, and then asked him to shut the door behind him to give her privacy from his brothers' conversation.

He was reluctant to leave her alone, and she let out a shaky breath when he finally left and she could no longer hear him or his brothers in the connecting bedchamber.

But then she made the mistake of glancing up, and she saw a gilt-decorated ceiling directly over her head. As she lowered her gaze, she noticed gold and crystal everywhere.

She moved around, peeking into a doorway that led to a spacious private sitting room. The room contained a long settee, empty bookshelves, and a large desk near the window.

The mantle in this room was bare, and she dug in her pocket for Algernon's wedding gift. Besides the ring on her finger, he'd given her a small toy figure of a woman that bore a striking resemblance to the one she'd lost here as a girl. It always astonished her that he remembered so many insignificant things about her, and she'd burst into tears on the spot at the time.

She backed out of the sitting room and faced her future as Duchess of Ravenswood, something she had trouble imagining on the journey here. How would she ever feel at home in this vast house with so much opulence everywhere she looked? The sheer grandeur of her bedchamber took her breath—and her composure—away.

She ducked behind a dressing screen and found water to splash on her face.

When she emerged, she felt slightly steadier when she looked around, but her father's trunks and her traveling case looked too shabby for anyone else to see.

She carried her lighter case into the large empty dressing closet she found, but on the way back for the trunks, she tripped and fell flat on her face on the Persian rug.

Her door burst open, and her new brother-in-law, Stratford, rushed into the room. "Maggie?"

"I'm fine, Stratford," she promised, pushing herself up to sit, and then taking his hand to get to her feet. "Just a moment of clumsiness."

"That used to be me," he admitted, grinning.

"Your head was always trying to go faster

than your legs could carry you." She glanced at the empty doorway he'd come through. "What were you doing, lurking at my door?"

He grinned. "Algernon said to wait for you."

"Am I expected somewhere?"

"No." Stratford shrugged. "But it's what they say when they want to exclude me from any serious conversation."

"That's terrible."

"No. Not really. Their discussions tend to be long-winded and I don't have the patience for them anyway. Algernon will tell me what I need to know in the end, or Jasper will." He smiled at her shyly. "So you are finally my sister."

She showed him her wedding ring. "To be your sister is the sole reason I accepted your brother's offer."

"Ha, unlikely," Stratford exclaimed, grinning back. "You're probably in love."

"I am."

"Good. Algernon deserves that after all he's been through," Stratford announced. "Can I help with anything?"

She glanced at the trunks and nodded. "You can pick those up for me and carry the left one to the sitting room, and the right one to my dressing closet."

"Happy to," he promised, but as he gallantly hefted the left, and heaviest, into the air, groaning, the bottom fell out of it. All her father's journals, along with the letters Maggie wanted to keep, were scattered across the floor...

Along with the unexpected glint of old metal and crumpled paper.

Maggie gaped at the mess. Stratford stared at the glittering contents on the floor, wide-eyed. "That was supposed to happen, wasn't it?"

"No." Maggie bent down and picked up a gold coin. She stared at it in shock, and then at the other money at her feet. "Does that trunk have a false bottom?"

"*Had* a false bottom," Stratford corrected, and crouched down opposite her. He hefted the broken trunk closer to look at it. Then he handed her a wad of banknotes that hadn't yet fallen out.

Maggie nearly swooned before she'd finished counting.

ALGERNON BARRELED THROUGH THE HOUSE, leaving Maggie behind to be watched over by Stratford, while his brothers went in search of their wives to share his good news. He nodded to anyone he passed, but was furious. He searched the house: the library, the morning room, his study, the dining room, and finally found Aunt Violet sitting on the back terrace, sipping tea alone.

"What is the meaning of this?" he demanded.

The old lady met his gaze, one brow raised regally. "The meaning of what?" she answered, in a manner that suggested amusement rather than fear.

Not surprising, since the dragon hadn't feared anyone in her very long life. Certainly not a duke.

He planted his feet and put his hands on his

hips. "When you said you would invite some of the family to visit Ravenswood, I did not imagine that you intended for all of them to come at once."

The old lady smiled sweetly and shrugged. "I cannot help it if you don't listen properly, boy. The family is not only your brothers. It is first, second, and third cousins, too. Well...you are all my family. They are yours, too, and wished to meet your bride, the one you rushed off to London to fetch."

He groaned and rubbed his hand across his brow. This was not how he hoped to reintroduce Maggie to Ravenswood. The palace was currently fit to bursting with Sweets. She would find it difficult to remember anyone's names.

According to Nash, every distant relative seemed to have come out of the woodwork to answer the dragon's summons. His household staff had scrambled with each new arrival to find room to fit them all. Some were sleeping in the halls.

The old lady sighed. "Now, now, boy. Sit down and calm yourself."

He gave her a hard stare and realized that she was never, ever going to apologize for this disaster.

Ravenswood hadn't hosted the entire family in years, and the last large gathering had been when he was young. He remembered when his mother had been alive, weaving through a crowded drawing room, trying—and failing—to find a seat to squeeze into. He was too old to perch on a windowsill now, and damned if he would just to give some cousin—third cousin—comfort they thought should be theirs.

The smaller gathering he'd arranged to celebrate his cousin Amity's marriage had been set in motion before he'd learned of the state of his financial affairs. He hadn't planned to host another house party for years because he could not spare the money.

"Seymour and I sorted everything out while you were away. There's nothing for you to worry about or do. It will be a tight squeeze for a while, but in a family as large as ours, that is to be expected."

"You might have warned me."

"I did."

He glanced around and then sat forward. "Do you have any idea the financial strain this puts the estate under?"

"Of course, boy. Of course, I do. But you were going to marry an heiress, and I want to see my family all together once more before I die."

He groaned under his breath. He had not married for money, and the dragon looked in perfect health, sitting here in the sun. "You're not dying."

"My dear boy, no one lives forever. Not even me. We get old. Our bodies don't work the way they once did. I mean, even *you* must feel it at your age."

He scowled at her again. He had only just turned eight and twenty. He was young—younger than his father had been when he was made Duke. However, he was older than his father had been when Algernon was born. That weighed on him a great deal, which was why having all the family here at such a time gave him nightmares. With all the family about, they might harass Maggie by talking about their offspring. Offspring she did not want.

"Now don't fret. You have your duchess to take over here soon. Lady Kent surely can manage a family gathering."

His stomach dropped. He had to tell her the truth, and now, before she made things worse. "My wife is not Lady Kent," he said slowly.

She froze momentarily, and then her cane stamped the ground beside her. "What did you say?"

"I chose a different bride in the end, Aunt Violet. I married her in London."

One of her canes tapped the ground. "Are you telling me you came home already married, but not to Lady Kent? That you married another without even telling your brothers about it or having them there beside you? Because I know they have not left the estate and they cannot keep a secret to save their lives."

"I did," he assured her.

Her lips twitched into an almost smile. "Whom did you marry, boy?"

"I married the woman I love," he announced.

"Nonsense! I will have her name this minute," she demanded, and the hair on the back of his neck rose at her obvious agitation.

"Margaret Black. Maggie," he informed her.

Aunt Violet's eyes narrowed dangerously. "Small, wild girl, obstinate disposition. The urchin who stole my cane?"

Suddenly, Maggie was by his side. "I could not allow you to strike Algernon then, and I will not tolerate it now."

Aunt Violet sat forward in her chair. "Come closer, girl."

"You are addressing my duchess," Algernon warned his aunt.

Maggie shushed him. "It's all right," she promised.

She approached the dragon without fear, but Algernon kept an eye on his aunt's canes, just in case they moved.

"You look older," Aunt Violet said.

"You look the same," Maggie replied. "Still old."

"Old enough to know you're going to cause trouble for the family," Aunt Violet complained.

Maggie lifted her chin slightly, a smile curling up the corner of her lips. "That is what ladies are made for, isn't it? Someone has to set a bad example."

"Indeed, they do. Sit down, girl," she demanded. "I preferred it when you were shorter."

"Perhaps later. I've barely arrived and there is so much to do," Maggie answered.

The old dragon actually accepted Maggie's refusal.

Aunt Violet nodded. "There will be a family dinner tonight in the garden. Everything is arranged, but should you desire changes made, please inform the housekeeper as soon as possible. The kitchen staff are hard at work even now. You will be presented to the family at dinner on Algernon's arm, and then they will finally all leave over the next few days."

Maggie inclined her head. "That is acceptable."

Algernon blinked rapidly, confused by what had just happened. Had Aunt Violet approved of his wife? Would there be peace in the house?

Maggie turned to him, kissing Algernon on the lips. "Join me upstairs when you're done here. I've some news that cannot wait."

Then she strolled back indoors.

Algernon stood about like an idiot until Aunt Violet stamped her cane. "Now about the matter I sent you to London for?"

He nodded and removed a paper from his pocket. "As requested. What did you do to the archbishop that he'd agree to provide a special license as soon as I mentioned your name?"

The old lady snatched the special license from him, then hugged the paper against her chest with her eyes closed. She did not explain her hold over the archbishop, but he understood her relief very well indeed.

Aunt Violet suddenly looked at him. "Tell no one about this yet."

Algernon nodded. "As you wish, Aunt, but perhaps the groom might like some warning of your intentions."

Her lips pursed tightly.

"He does *know* about this marriage license, doesn't he?"

She scowled.

"Oh, he doesn't." Algernon winced. "Does he want to marry you?"

"Of course he does. Or *did*, had my family not gotten in the way when we were young," she said, growing rigid with indignation.

Algernon had accepted the potential for scandal when his old butler married his crusty old aunt. "I'm certain he will come around once he learns he may stay at Ravenswood for the rest of his life with you."

It was a bold suggestion, which he'd given some thought to on the way home. Hadn't Aunt Violet announced she intended to remain at Ravenswood for the rest of her life? She could not be here without her husband, too.

A sudden smile lit up Aunt Violet's wrinkled face as she regarded him. "I knew you were my favorite for a reason."

Algernon couldn't hide his surprise. "Your favorite?"

"You made the right decision in the end. You married for love. Why else would I decide to make you my heir?"

He sat down quickly. "Your heir? Heir to what?"

"My estate, my other property," she advised him with another smile. "The value in the region of two hundred thousand pounds, at last count."

Algernon's jaw dropped. "What?"

The old woman chuckled, a dry sound he'd rarely heard from her. "Did you believe me cut off and penniless when I left Ravenswood and your awful father? I'm a great deal richer than he ever was, too."

He sat forward. "*How?* Father led me to believe quite the opposite."

She shrugged, her expression smug. "The

family liked me better than my older brother. When unmarried uncles and aunts died, they mentioned me in their wills. But never him."

He shook his head. "Two hundred thousand pounds is more than a mere mention."

"Perhaps, but they loved me best of all and disliked your wasteful father intensely. Everyone did."

Algernon completely understood their decision to leave his greedy father out of any wills.

And then he remembered the paper that he gave Aunt Violet, and his hope died. "If you are to marry, Seymour will take control of your estate."

"And he has already written his will, leaving all his worldly possessions to his beloved duke," Violet told him with a gentler smile. "I never suggested it, but Seymour has no family, and he adores you and his life here. Now...begone, *boy*, and find that wife of yours. I expect to see her holding your heir in her arms within a year."

Algernon clenched his jaw at the abrupt dismissal, and also to prevent any expression crossing his face that suggested that would never happen. Aunt Violet would find out Maggie's feelings about children eventually. For now, he'd rather have peace with her for as long as possible. Providing her with the means to marry her long-time love appeared to have softened her toward him a great deal.

He strolled back into the house, but once out of Aunt Violet's sight, he ran upstairs to find Maggie.

She was sitting on the floor in the duchess' rooms, her father's lesson books scattered all around her, an empty sherry glass in her hand.

When he drew closer, he caught sight of bright, shiny gold coins stacked around her in neat piles. "Maggie?"

"I always wondered what Papa did with his money. He sold the cottage when Mama died and never purchased another. He saved everything he earned and hid it in his trunks."

She reached for a stack of papers that he soon realized were currency when she handed them to him to look at. She got to her feet and headed to his bedchamber with her glass dangling from her fingers. He heard the clink of glass on glass as he flicked through the banknotes, attempting to count them. But then his eyes landed on other stacks that had been hidden behind Maggie's back, where she'd been sitting on the floor.

His eyes widened. "Good God!"

"I don't usually drink, you know, but I've had quite the shock just now," Maggie said, as she returned and handed him a second glass of sherry. "Cheers, husband. It seems you married an heiress after all!"

He let out a shaky breath. "My aunt just told me she has made me her sole heir."

"Did she really?" Maggie scowled. "How cruel of her to tell you only now."

"She had not made up her mind before I went to London to marry. She only decided when I came back with you as my duchess. Her estate is worth over two hundred thousand pounds."

Maggie tossed back her sherry as if it were water. "I'm glad for you, and us all, of course, but if she strikes anyone with those canes, I will take them away again and give her a rolling chair to move about with instead."

Algernon laughed softly, putting an arm around her back as he took away her empty glass to give her his untouched one. He waited till she'd finished that, too. "You never told me you took the dragon's canes away from her. She blamed me at first."

"I didn't tell you because you were a terrible liar then. You might have given me away and retrieved them too soon," she told him, putting her head against his chest. "We're going to be all right. The estate, your brothers, our horde of children stampeding through every room."

"We are indeed, my dear." He kissed her brow—and then looked at her sharply as her last words sank in. "What did you say about our children?"

Maggie sighed and patted his chest. "I lied about that before. Forgive me."

He turned her about and held her by the shoulders. "So you wanted children all along?"

"More than all the riches in Ravenswood," she promised, nodding quickly. "But only ever if they could be yours."

A smile broke over his face, slow and full of wonder. "Then we'd best get started," he murmured. Algernon kissed Maggie soundly, scooped her up into his arms, and carried her to his bed.

EPILOGUE

ALGERNON TOOK his hat from his head and wiped the sweat off his brow. He knocked on the weathered oak door just as it began to open. "Good morning!"

Laura stood there, a child on her hip. She blew a lock of hair from her eyes and scowled. "Yes, Your Grace."

He smiled, despite the frosty welcome, knowing that she was under siege and had been for days. "I only came to say that a litter of kittens arrived during the night. They are in the stables."

"Kittens. There are kittens. Kittens, every-one! Kittens," Nash sang in the background. "Come along, everyone. Let's go and see them."

Algernon jumped back as a horde of children —well, only six—and his brother charged out the door, with Roman Crawford chasing after them all. Roman and Amity had come to stay at

Ravenswood for the summer, and there had been few moments of true peace ever since.

"I thought a diversion might be appreciated," he murmured.

"You are the best brother. Here, take Violet for a moment."

Algernon took his niece immediately with the experience that came from years of practice as Laura disappeared back inside.

She returned, her arm about Amity, who waddled everywhere and had since the moment she'd arrived. Her stomach was huge, though her expression was serene.

"Still nothing?"

"Not a twinge."

"I'll send ice cream," he promised her.

"Algernon, ice cream doesn't bring about labor," Laura complained.

"Perhaps not, but it's always pleasant on a hot day like this while we wait."

"Send a barrel of it then."

He nodded and handed the child back. "I'll see what I can do. Call if you need anything."

He retreated from the door and headed around the side of the house and caught the first servant he found to deliver ice cream to his brother's apartment promptly.

He strolled across the rear of the house and caught the scent of smoke in the air. Not an unusual occurrence when Lord Aston visited the estate. He found the old man and his brother's wife, Win, quietly blowing smoke rings together. They were a quiet pair and never drew attention to how often they sat together. But occasionally, he noticed Aston patting Win's hand. Those moments always made his eyes sting a little. Win could never be openly referred to as the man's daughter. Not when she had once lived as his son...and had been replaced by an impostor to hide the shame.

Algernon did not disturb them but headed inside.

He followed the sound of Maggie's voice, as he always did, finding her inevitably in the Ravenswood library. Today, she had an audience. At her feet was his own family. Their tiny son, Crispin, and their dog, Lord George the Hound, both seemed to be enraptured by the sound of her dulcet tones.

Algernon could not blame them for their fascination and quietly entered the room. He carefully picked up his son from his crib and joined Maggie on the settee. He settled Crispin in the crook of his arm, rocked him a little, and adored him even more when his firstborn burped.

Their dog, a young hound, immediately jumped up to sit between him and Maggie.

Maggie patted the dog but continued reading

about the Romans who had built much of England's roads.

Algernon toed off his boots and wiggled his toes, footsore from traipsing about the estate all morning in search of a lost lamb. He'd much rather have been here, gazing adoringly at his wife and son.

The dog licked him, sensing somehow that he'd been overlooked.

"Yes, I adore you, too."

Maggie set her book down. "I'm positive that dog understands everything we say."

"And what we don't say out loud, as well," he suggested.

"You were gone a long time," Maggie murmured, putting the book aside at last.

"Lost sheep, and new kittens in the stables. And while I was out, I also learned there was some trouble at the Fuller residence in the last few days."

"Oh," Maggie said, breaking out into a quick smile she swiftly smothered again.

"Yes, I ran into Mr. Fuller in the field, and it seems his wife has threatened to bar him from her bed unless he supplies her with her own library."

"I see nothing wrong with a woman reading."

"He blamed *me* for their argument," Algernon said, glancing her way.

"What could you have to do with it?"

"Seems his wife now believes that books are a sign of a husband's love. She's been spending a lot of time with you lately, too," he noted, raising a brow. "What have you been saying to her?"

"I said nothing to inspire a mutiny in their marriage if there wasn't already cause for one," Maggie promised. "However, when I spoke of you, I did mention your respect for educated women several times."

"My approval?"

"Well, reading aloud to you does tend to make you amorous, dear!"

"Maggie, it is all of you that makes me amorous," Algernon professed. "Your body comes with a fine mind and a clever tongue."

"I know," she said, and her grin was decidedly impish when she glanced him over.

He knew that look. But he sighed, determined not to become distracted until after they had finished their talk. "Then why would Fuller's wife assume the quantity of books in their home makes any difference to the way he feels about her?"

"Mr. Fuller has a low opinion of his wife. It wouldn't hurt for her to broaden her interests a little further afield to prove him wrong."

"Maggie, that wasn't why he married her."

"Yes, I know exactly why he married her. He has made that quite clear. He only married her for her dowry," she complained. "She was an heiress, and he's so proud of having her funds in his pocket that he makes me ill. But the foolish woman seems to think he adores her."

"Maggie," Algernon chided. "I agree with you that all women should have an education, but I'll have the vicar here soon complaining that you're stirring up trouble. Our marriage is unique."

Maggie burst to her feet. "Are they still saying a duke set a bad example by marrying for love?"

Algernon stood, too, and set their son back in his crib. He approached his angry wife and smiled. "Yes, they do say we are terrible. The lot of us, too. But I, for one, am glad we married for the right reason, *before* we found your fortune. We're meant to be as happy as this."

Her eyes softened, and she threw her arms about him. "Yes, we certainly are happy."

A cane tapped loudly, and he released Maggie to face the darkest corner and the pair of chairs there. "Good morning, Aunt. Seymour."

But there was no one there to respond now. The tapping had only been in his imagination. He might have worried about that more, had others in his family not heard the same sound almost as often.

Maggie touched his arm. "I've felt them close all day, too."

He sighed and hugged his wife. Aunt Violet and Seymour had died not long ago, within days of each other, after a brief but happy union. He might never get used to not being called boy again or hearing those canes moving through the house.

"It's ready," Stratford suddenly called out.

Algernon pushed his sadness aside and headed toward the corner where a large canvas that his brother had been working on for months stood.

Stratford had not allowed anyone to see his new work, and Algernon's curiosity was high. He'd only seen brief glimpses in the early stages.

But when he saw the painting as a whole complete image, he was rendered utterly speechless.

Stratford had painted Algernon's portrait— and included everyone he loved in it, too.

He and Maggie were sitting close together, their son in his arms and a book on her lap. Their dog was at their feet, too.

But also, his family was featured behind them. Jasper and Sophie shared a chair. Nash and Laura appeared to be dancing, surrounded by their children. Roman and Amity were at a bookshelf, kissing. Aston was there with Win at his side, who was blowing a kiss toward her husband, the painter of the portrait, who could only be seen peeking around his canvas in a mirror's reflection.

But the biggest surprise of all was the pair seated and holding hands in the background, painted in a ghostly manner in that dark corner.

His eyes stung. "It was good of you to include Aunt Violet and Seymour."

"I hoped to earn us some goodwill with the dragon's restless spirit," Stratford whispered. "I hoped it would let her rest easy at last."

Algernon hugged his brother tightly and thanked him, and then invited Maggie and their son to join him to view their family painting.

"Remarkable," she whispered after a moment, reaching for Stratford's hand. "I'm so proud of you."

Stratford blushed as the family arrived and crowded around, heaping praise on their little brother.

Algernon held Maggie tightly in his arms, grateful for the gift of his son...but for her love and support most of all.

His life would never have been complete without her making every day better.

WILD RANDALLS SERIES

Engaging the Enemy ∼ Forsaking the Prize

Guarding the Spoils ∼ Hunting the Hero

*

SAINTS AND SINNERS SERIES

The Duke and I ∼ A Gentleman's Vow

An Earl of Her Own ∼ The Lady Tamed

A Necessary Wife

*

REBEL HEARTS SERIES

The Wedding Affair ∼ An Affair of Honor

The Christmas Affair ∼ An Affair so Right

*

MISS MAYHEM SERIES

Miss Watson's First Scandal

Miss George's Second Chance

Miss Radley's Third Dare

Miss Merton's Last Hope

ABOUT THE AUTHOR

USA Today Bestselling Author Heather Boyd believes every character she creates deserves their own happily-ever-after—no matter how much trouble she puts them through. With that goal in mind, she writes steamy romances that skirt the boundaries of propriety to keep readers enthralled until the wee hours of the morning. Heather has published over sixty regency romance novels and shorter works full of daring seductions and distinguished rogues. She lives north of Sydney, Australia, with her trio of rogues and a fluffy four-legged overlord.

Learn more about Heather at:
www.Heather-Boyd.com